NEGRO LOVE

By

Bobby Shaw

Copyright 2024 @ Bobby Shaw
All rights Reserved.

Dedication

Acknowledgement

Table of Contents

Dedication ii

Acknowledgement iii

Table of Contents iv

Introduction vi

Chapter One

    Understanding 1

Chapter Two

    A Foundation 11

Chapter Three

    True Love 18

Chapter Four

    The Decision 30

Chapter Five

    A Dream 45

Chapter Six

    Conversation 56

Chapter Seven

    Friendship 67

Chapter Eight

    Back to Georgia 78

Chapter Nine

    Family 88

Chapter Ten

    Christmas Week 99

Chapter Eleven

    Church - Free 109

Chapter Twele

    New Beginning 116

Chapter Thirteen 127

    Gambling .... **Error! Bookmark not defined.**

Chapter Fourteen

    To Know 134

Chapter Fifteen

    Years After College 141

Chapter Sixteen

    The Decision of Love 150

Introduction

Negro Love

Negro Love

Chapter One

Understanding

Jesse, a divorce daydreaming about Mellody asking him while they are sitting on the deck of their beach home. How the mugginess from the rain shower early during the day gives Jesse a feeling he can't breathe, imagining Mellody asking for a divorce.

As the ocean breeze comes upon Jesse giving air, giving calmness. Jesse now thinking it's just his imagination knowing Mellody loves him as he loves her. Still Jesse with sadness in his heart as he sits there thinking how he has put their marriage in an untrusting spot by indulging in gambling and losing a lot of money.

He knew betting on games was only a hobby of his, but durring this basketball season he got carried away betting on teams in the playoffs, losing a lot of money. Jesse knows he can't cover up this lost of money, and Mellody will find out he has been gambling, and there's nothing else to do, but to lose his silence and tell her the truth.

Jesse takes a deep breath getting his nerves up looking at Mellody, uttering he needs to tell her something. Mellody with her beautiful smile replying what is it sweatheart. Jesse takes another deep breath, swipering he lost a lot of money betting on basketball game.

Mellody smiling looking at Jesse asking how much. Jesse with silence, Mellody now asking loudly how much, how her smile turns to concernment. Jesse mubble twenty thousand dollars. Mellody eyes wide open shouting, say that again, Jessia with this uncomfortorable look mubble twenty thousand dollars.

Mellody throws her hand up, then gets up going into the beach home. Jesse feeling so much disappointment as he watch Mellody goes into the beach home, now with silence left nothing but for him to hear only the waves from the ocean hitting the beach shores, then back to the ocean.

Jesse sitting there though becoming teary eyes hating he had taken Mellody's beautiful smile, and turning it into disappointment, making her feel betrayed, heartbroken, knowing he had told her he had stop gambling.

Jesse wiped his eyes knowing he had to do something to put trust back into their relationship, for their marrige was the most important thing to him. The love Jesse has for Mellody never again wanting to see her beautiful smile turn to a look of concernment, nor hearing her silence as it was when she walked inside.

As the evening approaches Jesse seeing the sunset knowing how Mellody loves the evening on the beach, plus hearing the sound of the ocean while watching the sun disappear into the night. Jesse goes into the beach home asking

Mellody with a whisper, for her to take his hand, and walk in the sand with him.

Mellody still with disappointment on her face, as she looks at Jesse. Jesse can see the disappointment on her face, asking to talk to her about his problem with gambling. Mellody, noticed the redness in Jesse's eyes understanding he had been thinking. She gets up from her chair and takes his hand as they go walk on the beach.

Mellody listening to Jesse while they walk, yet still upset because of the money lost this time. She knew he gambled for a hobby, but never losing this amount of money before. Mellody knew when Jesse had absolutely won money previously, how she would get a gift, or two, but she was mostly upset because of the amount of money he lost is more than a hobby.

Jesse talking, understanding the words needing to come out of his mouth, explaining how his thoughts of not wanting to even lose a dollar turned into losing a few hundred dollars at first. Jesse takes a deep breath going on to say, only to doubling up on his betting not thinking of the thought he might not win what he had lost until it was to late.

Jesse looking at Mellody teary eyed making his case how he has been disapointed in himself for not only losing the money, but disapointed in himself for putting them in this situation, taking trust out of their marriage.

Mellody knows her love for Jesse has always been in a way she could overlook his flaws and would not judge him. She in thought, thinking for no human was perfect. Jesse feeling the tightness of her holding his hand. Jesse's feeling of grateful comes into his heart for having a woman with understanding and understanding of the words coming out of his mouth.

Now both are silent while walking holding hands reflecting on how they first met, Jesse thinking of how Mellody's smile brought happiness into his life. As when he first saw her, he felt something beautiful about her, and when her pretty face looked his way and smiled, that smile of hers melted his heart.

Yes, Mellody's smile brought joy to him, making him understand the true feeling of happiness. Jesse knew if he could get to know Mellody, his life would absolutely be complete.

As the sun is setting the shadows of two clouds, two clouds as though kissing, as though to say bye to the problems of yesterday. Jesse and Mellody turn around, they kiss, then they walk back to their beach home. As they are still saying nothing, both thinking when they first met.

Mellody a Second Lieutenant, a nurse at the military hospital. Jesse a First Lieutenant, military policeman, yet when he saw Mellody, he didn't know she was in the military. When he first saw her, she was in civilian clothes, wearing a beautiful black dress undeniable to notice. When Mellody noticed Jesse, he had a military haircut.

Again when Jesse first saw Mellody, not only how she was dressed but her beautiful face, her physical structure which was also undeniably noticeable and irresistible. He walked up to her and introduced himself, "Jesse," then he asked her name. Mellody looking at Jesse this dark skined man, how she was attracted to him, answering him, "Mellody."

Negro Love

Now back in front of their beach home the stars are shinning brightly, a full yellow moon so beautiful, the night breezes from the ocean give a little chill in the air. Mellody with a little shiver Jesse give her a hug to take the chill away, then a kiss, as she kissed him back now walking into their beach home.

Mellody goes to the kitchen to fix them something to eat. Jesse fixes them some mix drinks giving Mellody her drink, as he walks to the living room having a seat sipping on his drink remembering more when they first met.

Jesse as he was in thought remembering his first conversation with Mellody, how he would love a chance to get to know her by becoming friends. At the same time Mellody was in thought taking a sip of her drink, taking the chicken breasts out of the refrigerator she had season earlier. Mellody then cutting up an onion and an green pepper onto the chicken putting the chicken into the oven.

Mellody remembering how Jesse was so polite, how she didn't shun him off because of his manner of approaching her. Otherwise she would have done the same thing she done to most officers and civilian men who approached her rudely believing they could had gotten away with any kind of conversation with her.

Mellody smiling more as she takes another sip of her drink, then she starts making a salad to go with the chicken. Mellody remembering how she never gave out her contact information but because of how polite Jesse was she collected his number. Now with a little laughter she remembered telling him she might contact him, or she might not.

Bobby Shaw

Jesse flipping through the channels sipping on his drink smiling thinking how he waited for weeks, and the day came he got the call from Mellody, "Hi Lieutenant Jesse." Jesse, smiling the more, remembering getting that first call how hearing Mellody's voice gave him a feeling of happiness, everything stood still including his heart, his world ceases to revolve, words would not exist his mouth.

"Hello, are you there?" Jesse remembered Mellody asking. How he never knew the wait for her phone call would be so satisfying once he heard her voice. Jesse takes another sip of his drink remembering hearing Mellody conveying she wants to know him, too.

Mellody walks into the living room smiling, saying the food is ready, as Jesse gets up, walks to the kitchen. Both having a sit at the table as Jesse saying grace. Oh my! Jesse expresses how good the food smells looking at Mellody. Mellody smiling the more asking Jesse what kind of dressing he wants on his salad.

Jesse saying ranch dressing will be find, Mellody putting ranch dressing on his salad, handing it to him. She then hands the bake chicken to him. Soon as Jesse takes his first bite of the chicken, wow he express, going on to say this taste better than it smells, how this made Mellody feel even more special.

As Jesse eats still reminiscing when they first met.

Mellody was not a woman to be joked with, as she was a perfectionist but incredibly quiet, yet at times with a dry sense of humor.

Negro Love

Jesse licks his fingers as this made Mellody the happier knowing this meal was great. They finished eating going to the family room listening to some old school R&B, saying nothing he's holding her as she lays her head on his shoulder.

Mellody smiling remembering when they first met how she made Jesse wait while she did a thorough background check on him and had every vital information which was satisfying enough which led to her calling him.

Mellody had to be honest with herself, she had liked Jesse from the onset. Now with the hope whatever checks she made on him would turn out more positive than negative.

Mellody remembering after getting the results she wanted their first date to be at a very flamboyant restaurant, how she was glammed in her military uniform as she didn't have time to change into something more appropriate.

Jesse remembering Mellody beauty, even in her uniform, she was indeed a remarkable sight. At once, both knew they never wanted to be apart. How their eyes never to look elsewhere only to look at the menu to order, and while waiting for their dinner, eating some light snacks, how their conversation was engrossing and soul touching.

Jesse reminiscing how after dating for well past two years, he felt it was time to propose to Mellody, deciding to talk about this to his friend and fellow officer Sidney. Jesse went into Sidney's office telling him about his intention to propose to Mellody, to make her his wife. Sidney with excitement about the news, then Jesse showed Sidney a beautifully sculptured ring.

Jesse asked Sidney will he be his best man if Mellody says yes, well, well, Sidney saying, pretending to ponder on what he had been asked of him, he responded with a yes, he will be an honor to stand with him as his best man.

Jesse smiling thinking how much he misses his friend Sidney remembering what else Sidney had said, occurs Mellody will marry him. How Sidney asked him what is up with the word if, how Sidney had said no need for that word if, to had ever came out of his mouth, she goanna say yes, and he would be the best man.

Jesse remembering, he went into his office thinking how he had produced a plan to ask Mellody to marry him. Yes, Jesse shouted calling the nicest restaurant in the city making reservation for seven o'clock that tonight.

Once Jesse had made the reservation for a table and how he wanted it to be setup. Jesse was pleased knowing how the beauty of the river running through the city at night give a feeling of a romantic spot.

Jesse holding Mellody with a smile recollecting how he called her and asked her could she meet him at this nice restaurant around seven-thirty that tonight. He wanted to make sure everything was perfect before she got there.

Smiling Jesse thinking how he was feeling once he had gotten off the phone with Mellody the excitement he had, how he had pep in his step leaving his office then went to the cleaner getting his best dark blue suit out.

Jesse remebering when he made it home taking a shower, putting on his dark blue suit, looking in the mirror. How he saw himself so fly, loudly he shouting he's the man. Jesse put on some smell good leaving for the restaurant.

Mellody reminiscing how she got ready for the date that would change her life, but at the time not knowing Jesse was going to ask her to marry him, yet at the time she knew he was up to something asking her on a date during the middle of the week to one of the nicest restaurants in the city.

Jesse recalling when Mellody arrived, wearing this beautiful blue dress, his eyes was mesmerized, as the day when he first saw her. Jesse got up from the table overlooking the city, giving Mellody a hug, pulling out the chair for her to be seated. As she had a seat, she noticed two plates covered, two empty glasses and a bottle of an expensive wine. Mellody with a smile conveyed to Jesse, he was trying to be romantic.

Mellody feeling the warmth of Jesse as he is holding her, now Mellody thinking when she was seated, the covered plates, the empty glasses and the expensive wine but when she looked under the covered plate of hers. What she saw next surprised her, there was no prepared meal but a beautifully sculptured ring placed in the plate.

Mellody with a smile as she lay in Jesse's arm she can feel the warmth of Jesse's love, as did the night she felt that love, how that love had her eyes wide open, that love made her put her hand over her mouth. Yes, that night she gave Jesse a surprised look, as Jesse went on one knee, taking the ring looking at her.

Jesse can feel the warmth of Mellody's love as he hold her in his arm remembering what he said when he proposed to Mellody, how life has been beautiful since she has been in his life and he never wanted it to cease. How he took a deep breath and expressed he want to wake up every day with her in his arms. Mellody now smiling remembering Jesse, asking her to marry him, remembering how she softly said yes.

Chapter Two

A Foundation

Mellody and Grace getting off the school bus, Mellody looking at Grace, yelling she will race her to the house. Grace agreed, they started to run, Mellody saw where she was winning and the closer they got to the house, she slows down so Grace could win.

Once they had made it inside the house, Grace express, it smells good in here. The house smell of fried chicken, pinto beans, cornbread, when Martha, their mother, sees Mellody and Grace, she ask them to decorate the house, with the decoration on the couch in the living room.

Mellody and Grace got the fake snow fluff, the confetti, the balloons, putting everything up and down the hallway. Martha wants it special for John because today is his birthday. After putting up the decoration Mellody and Grace do their homework, after they had finished, two hours had passed when they comes from their room, asking if they could go ahead and eat.

With disappointment on her face, Martha express, sure, go ahead and eat. Martha goes on to say she will put their father a plate up in the oven. Grace asking Martha is she going to eat with them. Martha slightly smile replying, she ain't hungry right yet.

After Mellody and Grace had eaten, they goes back to their room going to sleep. Martha sitting on the couch teary eyes, in silents no television nor radio on, only a lamp on. Martha, feeling frustration, as she can feel the blood rushing to her head not knowing to be sad or mad, so she got up, goes look in on the girls seeing they are sleeping.

Martha goes back to the family room turning off the lamp, sitting back on the couch, waiting in the dark for John until she falls asleep. About an hour or so there was a knock at the door, then the doorbell rang. Martha turns on the lamp, now with excitement, this was John, he had lost his key. She goes an answer the door, what she sees is the Sheriff. Martha did not think anything, but John had gotten drunk.

Martha thoughts are because the Sheriff is a friend of John, he is bringing him home. Martha smiling at the Sheriff asking where's John. That is when the Sheriff explains, no, no, to Martha, he got some bad news and he wanted to see her in person to tell her what he is about to say.

Martha notice how the Sheriff had this sad, but serious look on his face, she ask with tears rolling down her cheeks, where's John? The Sheriff takes a deep breath and saying John died, his truck went over an embankment about three hours earlier.

The Sheriff sees the look in Martha's eyes, the shock, the pain of the news, making him become teary eyes while expressing he is deeply sorry. Martha give the Sheriff a hug, he left, and she closed the door going back to the family room sitting on the couch.

Martha, the hurt she was feeling, this unknown place, this pain, how her marriage to John was all her happiness, the happiness to never imagine being without him. Martha thoughts of the girls their father was gone, was gone forever. She got up from the couch, she goes and awaken them asking them to come in the family room so they could talk.

Once they all are in the family room Martha looking at Grace, then she looks at Mellody, tears coming down her face as Mellody and Grace asks what's wrong mommy. Martha saying their father died today in a car accident.

Mellody and Grace starts crying while sitting there and Martha she got up taking down the decoration in the hallway, going in the kitchen, throwing the birthday cake to the floor, then sitting on the floor crying, shouting why. Mellody and Grace comes into the kitchen sitting on the floor beside Martha as they all were crying and held one another.

After the funeral Martha, she never recovered from the death of John only later to pass away from a broken heart. How this made Grace and Mellody close throughout their life because they were their only family.

They go to the same HBCU that has a great nursing program whereas Mellody took ROTC to help her pay for school. She wanted Grace to take ROTC, but Grace was not the type that wanted to do early morning runs, or to sleep outdoors in twenty-degree weather, no, no, no that was not for her.

After graduating from college, now Mellody a lieutenant in the military and after Jesse had ask her to marry him. Mellody now at her place looking at a picture of her mother with this black flower dress and her father with a black suit on, how happy they were holding hands and smiling. Mellody thoughts of marriage, will it be the same kind of happiness, the same kind of love, as her parents.

Mellody became teary eyes wishing only if her father could walk her down the aisle and her mother could give her advice. She wipes her eyes shaking those thoughts away, now thinking her father will walk her down the aisle in spirit and she can hear her mother spirit say she will be a great wife. Mellody smiles getting in touch with Grace.

Both busy ladies, Mellody because of her tight military schedule and Grace, her working schedule. They need to plan the wedding together, to bring the best out of it, they met about four or five times during the planning and settling the rest through long phone conversations.

Mellody and Grace finally found the perfect date for the wedding which was favorable for both. Now Mellody was glad she could give Jesse a time so he could put his leave in for the wedding. Jesse had no family he could rely on because his father he never knew, and his stepfather he never like, plus his mother never took up for him against his stepfather.

Jesse when he was in high school, he left home staying with friends here and there, never settling down anywhere, but he knew college and the military would be his ticket to having the right and comfortable life he envisaged, yet how Jesse missed his mother but not wanting to contact her because of the dislike between his stepfather and him. He did not want to cause his mother any trouble, so, he stayed away hoping she would contact him.

His stepfather never liked him because he had the same handsome look as his father did. He was a spitting image of his father and that bothered his stepfather, so his stepfather made him go through hell.

A baby

Three years later Mellody delivering a baby girl at about four o'clock in the morning, on a Tuesday. Jesse was in the room while Mellody was in labor and then later when Mellody was laying in her bed holding the baby. Jesse could not describe or explain this feeling of love as he stood over the bed looking at Mellody and the baby.

Then Mellody sites up giving the baby to Jesse to hold, as he is holding the baby in his arms, looking into her beautiful brown eyes marvel at what he was seeing he expressing to the baby her existence is their responsibility to love and cherish forever. Yes, saying Mellody, smiling and agreeing with Jesse.

Forgiveness

A few years later Jesse started thinking about the parental love he never really had, after seeing how much he loves having a daughter, now he wondered if his mother ever had half this respect for him. This was making Jesse wanting to see his mother the more, as he had not set his eyes on her in years.

A year later Jesse decided to take Mellody and Paige back to his hometown to see his mother, no matter the feelings or reactions of his stepfather. Once they arrived, they got out of the car, and goes knocking on the door and this little girl only a year older than Paige answered the door.

Jesse introduces himself, Melloy, and Paige, the little girl leaving the door open running down the hallway hollering mommy there is some people at the door. Dorothy hearing Laken hollering as she was coming out of the kitchen, she asked what's wrong child. Laken pointing saying mommy there is some people at the door.

Bobby Shaw

Dorothy now in the hallway she could see the front door open then she sees Jesse, this lady, and a little girl. Dorothy puts her hands over her mouth as she became teary eyes, not believing what her eyes were seeing. It is Jesse her first fruit of her womb. How now she was screaming in tears of joy, how glad she was to see him as tears ran down her face.

Dorothy walks quickly to the door hollering come in, come on in this place. Jesse now teary eyes giving Dorothy a hug then he introducing Mellody and Paige. Dorothy hugged Mellody then she hugged Paige, Laken asks Dorothy who are these people, that's when Jesse picks up Laken saying he is her big brother.

Laken takes Paige by the hand as they goes into the family room to play, then Dorothy express she need to finish preparing dinner telling Jesse and Mellody to make themselves at home. Mellody asks if she can be of help, Dorothy smiling saying, yes, of course they have some serious catching up to do.

While in the kitchen they got to talking, Mellody looking at Dorothy conveying she was glad to have this opportunity to meet her and Laken, Dorothy smiling the more. About that time Big Ben walks into the house after getting off work asking loudly what is for dinner and whose car is in the driveway. Jesse sitting in the living room, now a little nervous after hearing Big Ben's voice.

Dorothy saying, the car in the driveway belongs to Jesse, Big Ben not thinking ask who, Dorothy said, Jesse, her son. Dorothy goes on to say to Big Ben, there are many things that wanted to be said to Jesse for years.

Big Ben was in shock as this was the last news he expected to hear that evening, but he summoned up courage and walks into the family room hoping to right his wrong of so many years even if it meant pleading on his knees.

Well, he did not have to go to that length as Jesse arose at the sight of Big Ben coming into the room, Big Ben stretched his hand out to give Jesse a handshake. Jesse never hesitated to receive it in warmth. Big Ben looks at Jesse seeing he was a man now, no longer that child he man-handled years ago in the name of jealousy or anger.

Big Ben over time realize Dorothy's loved him and he loved her, and he was wrong not to love her offspring, like he should had wholeheartedly. Big Ben realized with the heart break Dorothy carried over the years of missing Jesse, he should have shown fatherly love to Jesse not cold or mean treatments. Big Ben felt even worse and deeply sorry for all his past actions and mistakes as he looked at Jesse who was not just a grown man, but also a husband and a father.

Chapter Three

True Love

As Jesse stops thinking of the past, he looks at Mellody putting down his glass telling her how much he loves her. Jessie explaining how his life is nothing without her, and he will never disappoint her again.

Mellody puts her glass down and gives Jesse a kiss telling him how much she loves him, and she believes him. Mellody going on to say thanks for being the man he is by treating her sister as if she is his sister and having no problem with her, and her son coming to live with them.

Jesse gets up and take Mellody by the hand to the bedroom, as they lay on the bed, he touches her so lightly from her face to her feets. She kisses him on his neck rubbing his back, and then they made passionate love.

After making love Jesse holds Mellody in his arms, as Mellody begin to speak, how he listen to the sweet sounding words coming out of her mouth nothing negative only postive. Jesse listen to Mellody until she stops speaking, as they lay there looking at the ceiling until both falling asleep.

The next morning Jesse and Melody awaken with joy looking at one another smiling getting up taking a shower. After their shower they fixs some breakfast going sitting on their deck eating listening to the ocean, the waves back and forward, the breeze giving off a coolness. Mellody sits in Jesse's lap, and he holds her. Mellody feeling the warmth in his arms and Jesse feeling the warmth of her body.

As the day goes on, they start packing their things for the ride home, later that night, or early the next morning. Mellody calls Grace letting her know they will be home tomorrow sometime, then asking how is Paige. Grace saying like any teenager, she and Marcus are staying in their rooms only coming out to eat. Mellody laughs as they get off the phone.

Lost Love

Grace moody, bosses how she refused to treat Marcus her son with kid gloves, but when he turned sixteen, she gave him, his father new Impala SS. She knew without a man in his life things could go south quickly but when they move to Atlanta to live with family, she knew Marcus would be okay because her brother-in-law would be a good man in Marcus's life.

Marcus an ordinary young man living an exceedingly ordinary life, close to his mother, and now close with his Uncle Jesse, Aunt Mellody, and cousin Paige. Paige thinks of Marcus more of her brother than her cousin, and Marcus feels the same way. Grace and Jesse acting as siblings more so then in-laws the way they carry on sometimes.

Once Grace got off the phone with Mellody, she started to think about how good the marriage of Mellody and Jesse. Then she started to think of Sidney, how she was introduced to him by Jesse, how they hit it off immediately. The like she and

Sidney had for one another right from the start, not dating too long before they decided to get married.

Sidney knew how he felt, Grace knew also how she felt as they never wanted to be separated, and long distance was keeping them apart. They got to talking one weekend, saying to one another, how hard this was to be apart, and they need to take care of this distance immediately. At the same time both said, let us get married.

Immediately, Sidney pulled a ring out of his pocket getting down on one knee, asking Grace will she marry him. Grace shaking her head to say yes. Sidney got off his knee putting the ring on her finger. It was amazing as it fitted perfectly, Grace, she looked at the ring then she kissed Sidney.

After the kiss Grace asked Sidney how did he know her ring size, Sidney simply answered Mellody. Grace with a smile, with her hand up to her face looking at the ring asked Sidney how would he know she would say yes, Sidney again with a smile answering, Mellody.

Grace looking at her ring as she walks upstairs looking in on Paige seeing she was asleep. Then she goes back downstairs to the basement apartment looking in on Marcus seeing he was asleep also. Marcus was incredibly young at the time Sidney passed away, how he never got the chance to know his father.

Grace, she goes to her room putting on her night gown, going into her nightstand getting the book she had started reading. As she lays in her bed reading the book holding back her tears, she stops reading and starts thinking back of Sidney.

Grace thinking how Sidney did not reenlist in the military when his time was up, getting a manager job at this paper mill in this small town in Northern Alabama. She knew he cared about her deeply and the love he gave her was unconditional as was hers love for him. He was the protector of her feelings, the provider of her needs, he vowed never to break her heart.

The day came he did, one fatal morning, but it was no fault of his. Sidney going to work one black ice cool morning, driving on a two-lane road. How he participated in a ghastly car crash, all efforts to save him were unsuccessful as he died at the accident never to return home to his lovely wife and son.

Grace now became teary eyes remembering saying to Sidney that fatal morning, wakeup, wakeup shaking him to get up out of bed to go to work. Remembering Sidney saying today was a good day to stay home, remembering she said bills cannot get paid taking the day off. Then remembering she got up going to Marcus room looking in on him then waking to the kitchen cooking some breakfast.

How Sidney got up, and got ready for work then walking down the hallway seeing Marcus picking him up walking into the kitchen. After eating breakfast Sidney kiss Marcus on the forehead then giving Grace a kiss saying goodbye, stressing he will be straight home and have a taste for her fried chicken. Sidney leaving the house going to his old truck getting the ice off the windshield, then getting in his truck going to work.

Grace after all these years still with the pain, the guilt of Sidney death. Grace still asking herself why did she not let him sleep in and take the day off. They had no problem with bills, plus money in the bank. Sidney had just bought him a new SS Impala, he only drove it from the dealership to their home. Only the thought of Sidney being in Heaven give Grace a reason to survive.

Now tears flowing down Grace's eyes feeling how long the days were, and the nights were even longer, the only way she can make it, and the only way she can take it was to know he was here in her heart.

Grace started back to reading this book Mellody had giving her, coming to a page where she had a letter she had written to Sidney after his funeral. Grace unfolds the letter and started to read the letter.

I awaken this morning, I awaken to you not being here with me, not because you are away on a trip, but because you are gone physically from this world, I awaken with a prayer, giving thanks I can see another day, I awaken with a prayer I can make it through this day, I am confident you would be happy I can be strong for our son.

I awaken wishing I could be where you are this day, but I know you would not want such. How this day I am blessed, yet unhappiness. I awaken to the sounds of the birds whistling in harmony wishing it were the sound of your voice whispering with softness in my ears saying, good morning. I awaken to memories, the memories that were ours.

The memories of the times we laughed non-stop till we had tears running down our cheeks. I miss awakening to the beauty I saw every day, the beauty of you. I awaken to memories never to be forgotten, only to be remembered forever as they will keep me going. For just the memories of you and what you gave me I can make it through these tough and lonely times. Saying goodbye for now.

After reading the letter Grace wipe her tears away thinking how grateful to had love Sidney for the time she did, plus giving her a son. How grateful she was for Jesse to have introduce her to Sidney, plus now having no problem with her and Marcus living with them. Grace puts the letter back on the same page where she had stop reading the book she was reading.

For some reason when reading this book, she would always start over reading to the page she bookmarks with her letter to Sidney, and that was as far she had ever gotten in this book. She closes the book putting the book in her nightstand seeing the letter Sidney's mother had written to her. Grace holds the address to her heart remembering how Sidney never talk about his parents.

Sidney

Every time Grace would bring Sydney's parents up, he would dance around the conversation. She was aware of his usual dance when she asked about his parents, but this one time she wanted answers after having their son, Marcus.

Grace remembered pleading with Sidney about wanting to know who were his parents. Remembering how Sidney treated the question in the usual manner, with silence as if no question were asked. Grace also remembered when she lost her cool asking Sidney was it her, was he ashamed of her.

Remembering Sidney making it clear, he is not ashamed of her, but still Sidney with this shameful look on his face saying he just does not want to talk about his parents. How Grace angrily got off the couch and prepared to storm out the room when Sidney's voice halted her saying okay, okay don't go. Sidney taking a deep breath uttering he was ashamed of his mother and father to the point he is ashamed of himself to contact them.

Grace then remembering Sidney telling his story of growing up, how he grew up on a farm, and his grandfather and grandmother were very respected. How his aunts and uncles were also respected, but not his mother and father. His mother and father got married because his mother got pregnant with him. How the day she found out she was pregnant, that night she told his father, and they ran away, but only to come back the next day going to the preacher's house getting married.

Grace with a tear now remembered Sidney explaining how one of his cousins always talking and teasing him, saying to him if it were not for their granddaddy his daddy would be nothing.

How Sidney at the time he did not understand, plus looking at how his aunts, and uncles were living a glamorous life because they always dressed nicely and were educated. Yet, his mother always in a plan dress, and his father always wore overalls, and they did not finished school.

Grace with more tears remembering Sidney shouting poor mom and dad, how they put up with him, and once he left for college, he never looked back. After graduating from college, he went into the military.

Only after Sidney's funeral when Grace was packing up Sidney's things, she found a letter with Sidney's parents address. Sidney had written a letter he never mails to his mother and father. Grace remembers opening the letter, and what the letter was saying. Sidney had written how he was sad about how he treated them, and how they put up with all his ways, never getting mad at him even when he would put them down.

Grace with new tears remembering how she felt so heartbroken the more Sidney had pass away, and did not send the letter. She remembered she got a pin and paper, writing to Sidney's parents, about him passing away, putting it with Sidney's letter mailing the letters to his parents.

Grace, as she was sitting on the side of the bed, she started reading the letter Sidney's mother had written her back. "I notices this letter addressed to me and Lewis, and it was not from around here, so while walking back to the house I open the letter. By the time I had gotten to the steps, I had to sit, and while reading the letter, I could not move, yes, sitting there crying as loud as I could. Lewis had come from the field for lunch, seeing me sitting on the steps crying, wondering what is going on, and then he asked me, what is wrong? I gave him the letter shouting our son is gone, our son is gone.

With tears in his eyes, Lewis reading more of the letter and said, Shirley, he left us a grandson, plus a wife now our daughter. Still crying, I said we need to see our daughter and grandson. When we started reading the letter Sidney had written us, but never sent, we hug one another and look to the heaven saying, we love you too, and we never stop loving you."

Grace putting the letter back into the nightstand, now laying in the bed looking up at the ceiling remembering going to visit Shirley and Lewis for the first time. Grace laughing stilling looking up at the ceiling remembering when making it there this one Friday on the bus to Shirley and Lewis Georgia hometown how small the town was, even smaller than where she was living in Alabama.

Catching a cab, and the cab driver putting their luggage in the trunk of the cab asking her where she would like him to take her and her son. Grace saying to Alvin and Sallie's farm, and then the driver said, he knows that place well. Alvin and Sallie are his in-laws.

Grace remembered asking the cab driver who was he, Charles he said. Then he asked her what kin were she and her son to Alvin and Sallie. Grace with a smile remembered with proudness saying she was married to Sidney, Lewis, and Shirley's son. Then Grace remembering Charles asking her was married, and with a little sadness in her voice telling Charles, Sidney died in a car wreck.

The sadness Grace remembering hearing in Charles's voice, stressing he was so sorry knowing how much Lewis and Shirley was proud of him. Remembering when Shirley told Lewis she was pregnant and that night they ran away but came back the next day going to the preacher's house getting married.

Once that conversation was over, going from the small town to the farm was about a fifteen-minute drive, Charles getting out of the cab hollering they are here. Charles gathering up their luggage, still hollering mom, dad, Shirley, Lewis, company.

Grace smiling the more remembering Shirley running out the house after hearing Charles said, y'all got company, then seeing it was her and Marcus. She had such a smile on her face, giving her a big hug, and then Marcus an even bigger hug.

Grace remembering having a feeling of how if her mom were alive, how that hug would have felt. Shirley kissing all over Marcus, and then said come on in the house, come on in this place. Once in the house, Charles took their luggage to a bedroom upstairs.

Shirley took Grace and Marcus to the back porch where Alvin and Sallie were sitting looking over their land. Shirley introduces Grace and Marcus to them, she said this is y'all Grandfather Alvin, and Grandmother Sallie.

Shirley knew to introduce Grace that way because Alvin and Sallie believe once in the family it is just family. Alvin said darn tootin' this little boy looking like his grandson, from his son. Alvin and Sallie got up and gave Marcus all the hugs and kisses he could stand.

About that time, it was lunchtime, Lewis coming in from the field for lunch. Lewis now walking into the house, but he did not smell anything cooking yelling, where is everyone? Shirley yells back, reckon they be on the back porch.

When Lewis walked on the back porch, the first person he saw was the perfect likeness to Sidney at that age, he knew at that moment this was his grandson. Lewis grabbed Marcus hugging him, then seeing Grace with his arm around Marcus introducing himself, Lewis. Grace with her beautiful smile turned to a tear as she looked at Lewis eyes seeing Sidney.

Lewis asked Grace still with his arm around Marcus asking Grace was she all right. Grace wiped her tear away saying to Lewis she was sorry, but he looked exactly like Sidney. Lewis, still with his arms around Marcus, walk to Grace giving her a hug, saying they miss Sidney too.

Grace still staring at the ceiling, falling asleep feeling kind of guilty because she and Marcus hasn't been back in years to see Lewis and Shirley even though now, they live in Atlanta.

Grace said aloud she got to do better about Marcus seeing his family. Grace remembering the last time she saw them Lewis and Shirley they were taking her and Marcus to the bus stop, remembering Lewis asked her did she need anything or did she need anything for Marcus. How she answered, no, but thanks, remembering Shirley with tears in her eyes conveying, they are family, come to visit anytime, there no invitation needed.

Grace trying to fall asleep finally, Grace falls asleep waking the next morning with the smell of breakfast, Grace got up then said a prayer then walk upstairs only to see Paige and Marcus in the kitchen cooking breakfast. Then about that time Mellody and Jesse walks into the house.

Jesse takes their bags to the bedroom while Mellody goes into the kitchen saying something smells good in here, as did Jesse walking into the kitchen. Paige then said breakfast is ready, as they all sit down to eat, and Grace bless the food.

After breakfast Marcus goes outside and cut the grass, as Paige washes the dishes, Jesse, Mellody, and Grace goes sit in the family room conversating. Jesse winks his eye at Mellody saying to Grace breakfast was good, and he glad she did not cook it. Grace threw a pillow at Jesse, hitting Mellody. Mellody threw a pillow back at Grace only to knock a lamp over.

About that time Paige walks by the family room going upstairs to her room and she sees the lamp knock over picking it up, and putting it back on the end table saying nothing only to feel the fun these grown folks were having acting like children.

Later Marcus comes into the house after cutting the grass and every time Marcus cuts the grass Jesse wants to give him some money. Marcus was like no, that is his responsibility, plus he is thankful for him being the uncle he is.

Jesse gives Marcus a handshake saying how proud Sidney would have been of him. Marcus, smiling, going to his room. Paige could hear Marcus talking to Jesse knowing Marcus was going to his room. She left her bedroom using the backstairs going and knocking on Marcus's door asking can she come in, Marcus is like occurs. Paige walks into the room, asking Marcus can she tell him something and he want judge her. Marcus is like he would not, nor will ever judge her.

Paige said she like girls, and if she tell her mother and father, they will look at her differently. Marcus with a look of encouragement at Paige saying Uncle Jesse, and Aunt Mellody, they will never look different at her because of the people they are. Jesse gets up from sitting on the bed giving Paige a hug saying thanks for trusting in him.

Paige with a smile saying no matter what happen in life she will always have trust in him. This put an even bigger smile on Marcus face. Marcus asking Paige when is she going to tell Uncle Jesse and Aunt Mellody. Paige said in time, in due time.

Paige walks out of the room, as Marcus lay across the bed looking at this magazine of the new Jordan coming out thinking on how he can get enough money without asking his mother for the money. Marcus producing, he will work all the hours he can at the fast-food place.

Chapter Four

The Decision

Marcus in class falling asleep because he had worked extra hard on the night shift at the fast-food restaurant the night before. He wants to earn extra money to get them new Jordan coming out next week plus to ask Stacy out on a date.

The teacher sees Marcus asleep calling him out conveying with a loud voice the next time he catches him sleeping in this class, he will send him straight to the principal's office. Everyone in the class starts to laugh, everyone but Hakeem.

After class Marcus best friend Hakeem asks why was he asleep during class. Marcus smiling explaining to Hakeem, he got to get them new Jordan coming out next week plus have some money to ask Stacy out the same weekend.

Hakeem with this look of an idea on his face saying, hmm, putting his hand on Marcus shoulder. Marcus is like what is up, Hakeem express he can get them Jordan for him when they come out next week, but he needs a favor. Marcus asks what is the favor, Hakeem replies, dropping a package off for him. Marcus asking with curiousness in his voice, all he got to do is drop a package off, Hakeem smiling with yes, for real bro.

Then Marcus asks, what is in the package, Hakeem smiling the more with, do not worry about what is in the package, taking his hand off Marcus shoulder asking him do he want them, new Jordan. Marcus saying, let him think about it, he will get back.

Hakeem gives Marcus their usual handshake, then walks away, Marcus thinking about how fly and sophisticated Hakeem looks and dresses. Marcus though about Hakeem getting him them new Jordan the rest of the day.

While Marcus and Paige are riding home, Paige asking Marcus why do he hang around Hakeem, he's trouble. While Marcus is driving listening to Paige, he cannot but to think of doing Hakeem this favor to get them Jordan plus having some money to ask Stacy out the next weekend if he delivers the package.

Once they made it home Marcus drops off Paige going straight to work. Once he made it to work, his boss hands him his check, Marcus looks at his paycheck, seeing it is enough to get them new Jordan coming out, but nothing else.

Marcus folds his paycheck putting it into his pocket then starts working the grill, flipping burgers thinking of Hakeem's offer. Marcus thinking how much he wants to take out Stacy but still wondering what is in the package he will have to deliver and to whom.

The next morning when Marcus and Paige made it to school Hakeem standing by Marcus locker speaking what up shorty to Paige, as she walks by Hakeem saying nothing. Hakeem giving Marcus their usual handshake, with a smile Marcus saying yes he will deliver the package.

Marcus a little nervous about what he has to deliver but he wants them Jordan plus some extra money to ask Stacy out. Hakeem then gives Marcus their usual handshake saying great bro. Hakeem then gives Marcus a piece of paper with his address telling him to quickly visit after school and he will give him the package to deliver.

Once school was over, Marcus drops Paige off at home, then he goes straight to Hakeen's place. Hakeem with his own place as he is a year or so older than Marcus, due to negligence on Hakeem part, he had issues with his education falling back a grade or two, and now Marcus classmate.

Marcus pulls up to the address Hakeem had given him getting out of his car looking at the piece of paper seeing which apartment is Hakeem. Marcus knocking on Hakeem's door, Hakeem looks out the peek hole letting Marcus into his place.

This is Marcus first time over to Hakeem's place, once Marcus is in the apartment both giving their usual handshake, now Marcus he is looking around, saying Yo man! Nice place. Hakeem with a smile saying ya no, how we do, giving Marcus another handshake, then offering Marcus a beer. Marcus politely saying no to the beer, asking for the package.

Hakeem goes get the package and hands it over to Marcus, giving him the directions on where to drop off the package. Marcus listening to the direction taking the package giving Hakeem their usual handshake. Marcus then say to Hakeem he will see him in class Monday and not to worry about the delivery of the package.

Marcus following the directions Hakeem had given which led to an apartment building close to where Marcus works. Marcus pulling up into the parking lot nervous, now thinking to himself, what has he gotten himself into then saying, oh well, since he had agreed to deliver the package, and he is already on the job.

Marcus gets himself together, gets out his car with the package then walks to the door of the apartment and knocks. Luckily, a lady holding a little girl answering the door putting a smile on his face. A special feeling comes across Marcus and also the lady, as they look at one another, both having sandy brown eyes, but neither saying anything. Marcus gives her the package saying this is from Hakeem, she expresses thanks closing the door.

Marcus breathes a sigh of relief as he hurriedly going down the stairs, jumping into his car, and driving to work. Because he is about ten minutes late, that spells trouble between him and his boss, that's what Marcus was trying to prevent happened.

Once in the building, his boss seriously, loudly spoke, do not be late again, the next time go ahead and find another job. Marcus saying nothing, but he has this look he is sorry for being late to work.

Monday

Monday before school Hakeem comes up to Marcus in front of his locker and hands him the money for the new Jordan saying, if he wants to make some real money, and want to stop being harassed at that fast food place let them talk.

Marcus saying thanks for the money asking, real work, real money. Hakeem smiles with a yes, real work, real money and how he heard of his boss treated him because of being a few minutes late. Hakeem smiling saying that package he had delivered for him was a trial to see how much he could be trusted.

Marcus smiling conveys he can always be trusted, then Hakeem expresses now he knows because the package he gave him had a thousand dollars to delivered to his baby and her mother. Marcus now smiling the more, expressing he might take him up on making some real money. Then Marcus give Hakeem their usual handshake going to class.

Marcus in class daydream about now having enough money to ask Stacy out on a date. So, after the next couple of classes, at lunchtime Marcus sees Stacy sitting there at the lunch table with her friends.

Marcus walks up to the table where Stacy and her friends are sitting smoothly saying hello to them. He then looks at Stacy asking her can he have a few seconds of her time to speak with her. She looks at her friends, and then looks at him smiling saying sure. Stacy stands up, and she sits back down saying his few seconds are up.

Marcus with this look of sadness walking off when Stacy saying wait, wait, she was just joking. Marcus sad look turns to a big smile, and he then in front of her friends he ask her if she would like to go on a date with him.

Stacy stares hard at him then look at her friends as they smile and then she looks at Marcus saying sure. Then she asks him for his cell phone Marcus gives her his cell phone then she put her number in his cell phone, and about that time the bell rung. Lunch was over, and while walking away Marcus express, he will call her tonight, Stacy looks at him with a smile walking away.

After School

After school, while Marcus and Paige are riding home from school Paige with a big smile expressing she saw him talking to Stacy at lunch. Then Paige goes on to say Stacy is one of the smart ones at this school, she is a keeper, Marcus smiles saying nothing.

Once home Marcus runs straight by Grace as she is leaving for work going to the kitchen to gets him a snack because he was hungry from missing lunch. Paige is laughing and Grace ask Paige why is she laughing plus why is Marcus running by her without speaking.

Paige with more laughter saying because he is hungry, he did not eat lunch today trying to talk to this girl. Grace starts to laugh as she walks into the kitchen asking Marcus was it worth it, Marcus kiss Grace on the jaw saying yes, mother.

Then he starts eating a snack fast, as Grace smile leaving for work, she is the night nurse in charge. Later that night Marcus calls Stacy asking her what she like as far as food and movie so he can get an idea where to take her on this date.

Saturday Night

When Saturday night comes Marcus with his new Jordan on and money in pocket, he goes to Stacy house to pick her up, realizing she lives around the street from him. Marcus ringing Stacy's doorbell when her mother comes to the door, and he introduces himself. Stacy's mother asks him to come into the house as she looks him in the eyes, then she had to look away. About that time Stacy comes down the stairs Marcus can see Stay is more beautiful than he had ever seen her at school before.

As they leave Stacy's mother expressing have a good time. Marcus can tell Stacy is on another level while listening to her talk. That night after their date Marcus dropping Stacy off at home, walking her to the door giving her a kiss on the cheek.

Walking to his car thinking he needs to make some money, more than he is making at the restaurant to keep Stacy happy.

Monday

Monday morning riding to school Paige asks Marcus how did his date with Stacy go. Marcus explaining she is on another level then him, she was talking about her future. Paige asks Marcus what about his future, what is he going to do after high school. Marcus saying nothing, only silence the rest of the ride to school, but now only thinking about making money with Hakeem.

Before class Hakeem comes up to Marcus at his locker, asking him will he ride with him after school, he got someone he wants him to meet. Marcus saying okay but first he has to drop Paige off at home. Hakeem saying cool drop her off then come by his place.

During classes all morning all Marcus can do is think of how much he wants to know Stacy the more. In his class right before lunch his teacher notices Marcus in a daydream calls on him to answer a question but Marcus could not answer the question, the teacher saying pay attention. About that time the bell rung, Marcus can't wait for lunch to see Stacy.

Marcus when he goes to the lunchroom there Stacy is sitting with her friends. When she sees Marcus coming into the lunchroom, she raises her hand for him to come to where she is, and with a smile Marcus comes to her table. In front of her friends, she express to Marcus she enjoyed last weekend and if they can do it again. Marcus with a bigger smile saying occurs.

After School

Negro Love

After school Marcus drops Paige off going straight over to Hakeem's place, knocking on the door, Hakeem looking out the peek hole seeing it is Marcus letting him into his place. Once in Marcus looking around still amazed how Hakeem lives. Hakeem gives Marcus a handshake asking him is he ready to ride. Word up Marcus saying as they left Hakeem's place.

They walk about a block down the street to a parking deck, walking up to this nice car, a new 3M BMW. Marcus is like yo man nice car who is this. Hakeem saying word, it is his car going on to say he tries to stay low key at school and not cause unnecessary attention.

After getting into the car Hakeem opens his glove compartment, ensuring that all the paperwork is correct with his fake I.D., and matching registration. Hakeem's I.D. has him a lot older than his actual age so if he gets pull over by the police, everything will correlate enough to match the kind of car he is driving, plus making him look older driving the type of car he is driving.

As they drive away from the parking deck Marcus ask where are they going. Hakeem looks at Marcus then express do not worry about that, just enjoy the ride. They drove for about an hour or so with traffic and pulled up to this gated community, and Hakeem puts his code in as the gate opens, driving two blocks in front of a lovely house.

As they got out of the car, Marcus asks who lives here, Hakeem smiles then saying his sister, she used to be a stripper, but now she owns a strip club. Hakeem opens the door, goes in, then goes straight to the kitchen to make him a sandwich, asking Marcus if he wants one. Marcus like word, and about that time, Hakeem sister comes into the room looking like a supermodel.

Marcus looks at Hakeem's sister, and his thought to himself, how beautiful she looks, as he has never seen such a beautiful woman in his entire life. Hakeem's sister hugs him, treating him more like a son than her little brother because she raised him. Their mother passed away right after giving birth to him.

Hakeem's sister Kelly asks who is this young man, Hakeem saying this is his friend Marcus. Hakeem goes on to explain, Marcus is the only guy he can trust, he is loyal, and if something ever happens to him, he can take his place. Marcus looks at Hakeem with this scared look hearing what Matthew just said.

Kelly sees the look on Marcus face expressing everything is cool there's nothing going to ever happen to Hakeem, walking over giving Marcus a hug. Hakeem finished making him and Marcus sandwiches as the three of them sits at the table. As Hakeem is eating, he is saying he tried to tempt Marcus with money, and he never took a thing from him.

As Marcus is eating his sandwich Hakeem looks at Kelly expressing, Marcus can be of good help if he wants in, now Hakeem looking at Marcus stressing real money. Marcus saying word, and Kelly expressing welcome to the family. Kelly looks at her watch saying she got to leave for the club telling Hakeem to lock up when he leaves. Hakeem express they are leaving now he just wanted to bring Marcus by to introduce him.

On the ride home Marcus seems a little nervous, as Hakeem is driving talking, but getting no response from Marcus. Hakeem looks over at Marcus and can see the nervousness in Marcus eyes. Bro! Hakeem saying everything is going to be okay, now with a smile Marcus saying word up. As they talk and laugh the rest of the ride home.

Once they made it back to the parking deck, and Hakeem park his car, Marcus looks at his watch stressing he needs to get home before his uncle or aunt notices. Marcus and Hakeem run the block to Hakeem's apartment. Once there they shook hands as Marcus gets in his car and takes off for home.

Once Hakeem made into his apartment Kelly calls him asking Hakeem to bring Marcus over to the house for lunch the coming Saturday, so she can introduce Frank to Marcus. Hakeem saying okay getting off the phone with Kelly, then Hakeem picking out what he is going to wear to school tomorrow. Then he calls Shelia asking her to put Zoie up to the phone so he can say he love her.

Marcus making it home Jesse and Mellody are sitting on the couch watching television when Marcus walks into the house. Mellody asks Marcus do he wants something to eat, Marcus saying no thanks, he had eat something at work. Then Jesse expressing keep up the good work, working and going to school never hurt anyone. Marcus saying goodnight going downstairs to his room.

The next morning Paige and Marcus are riding to school when Paige express to Marcus, she heard the lie he told her parents last night because she knows he didn't go to work because he never change into his work uniform.

Marcus laughs saying whenever have he ever wore a uniform. Paige laugh reaching in the back seat getting Marcus work jacket saying this here. Paige then express this has been seating in the same place since yesterday. Marcus looks a Paige smiling saying nothing else.

Hakeem standing by Marcus locker when Marcus walks up giving him their usual handshake. Hakeem saying Kelly wants them to come over this Saturday for lunch so she can introduce him to Frank, her boyfriend. Marcus is like word, Hakeem saying word.

Saturday

Saturday morning Marcus wanting to spend time with Grace because he barely gets to see her during the week. Marcus gets up early sitting in the family room waiting for Grace to get off work. Grace walks into the house tried, sleepy, and Marcus gives her a hug asking her do she wants to go to a movie with him and Stacy tonight.

Grace smile expressing that will be great, but she would rather stay home and watch a ole school gangster movies in the theater in the basement. Marcus gives her another hug saying okay mother, then asking can he ask Stacy to come over and watch the movie with them. Grace smiling saying occurs the more the marrier.

Paige walking down the stair as Mellody is coming out of her bedroom, both hearing Grace and Marcus conversating about watching a ole school gangster movie asking can they watch the movie with them. Marcus smile saying yes, a family date tonight.

Grace goes downstairs to her bedroom as Mellody and Paige goes to the kitchen. Marcus goes downstairs to his room and calls Stacy asking her would she like to come over tonight and watch a ole school gangster movie with his family.

Stacy, still half-asleep expressing that will be great asking Marcus what time. Marcus saying around six asking Stacy if she want him to come pick her up. Stacy with a little laughter saying no, she can drive around the street.

Later that morning Marcus goes over to Hakeem's place, and they jog to the parking deck getting in Hakeem's BMW driving to Kelly's place. Once Hakeem and Marcus had made it through the Saturday morning I-75 south traffic to Kelly's place, going into the gated community Hakeem parks by this new Mercedes-Benz G 63AMG.

Marcus looks at the Mercedes-Benz saying nice this him one day. Then Marcus asks Hakeem who ride is this, and Hakeem with a smile saying Frank while walking into the house. Frank and Kelly are sitting on the couch conversating when Hakeem and Marcus walks into the house.

Kelly express to have a seat, then Kelly getting straight to the point asking Hakeem how much do he trust Marcus. Marcus with this curious look, then Hakeem saying he trust Marcus as if he was his brother.

Kelly with a smile expressing that is what she wanted to here, going on to say, she wants them to learn the business, to understand how to cover every angle in every way. Frank jumps into the conversation saying because no matter how smart one may think he is, he still needs to learn more.

Marcus and Hakeem listening to Frank talking, as Frank explaining learn how to deal with anyone in any situation, like when to take a loss, not to get upset because it will cost more eventually.

Frank smile then explaining more still deal with the one who gave the lost just be smart about how to deal with that person. Frank goes on to say learn how to get respect in a way one does not have to be forceful, but still powerful.

Kelly then introduces Marcus to Frank, Marcus giving Frank a strong handshake. Frank looking Marcus in the eyes thinking back in the day his cousin Sidney had them same sandy brown eyes and the same kind of handshake.

Then Frank, he looks more at Marcus asking who is his mother and father, Marcus saying his mother is Grace and he never knew his father because he passed away when he was young. After lunch Marcus saying he needs to get home, then Kelly giving him a hug and Frank giving him another handshake.

After they had left Frank express to Kelly there is something special about Marcus, he can take his son Alphonso place, but he need to check out something first. Yes, Kelley saying Marcus seem smart enough to learn from Hakeem, because unlike Alfonso who care about show boating bring attention to himself, Hakeem don't, and Marcus seem that way also.

On the ride home Marcus saying he will not do anything to disappoint Kelly nor Frank, Hakeem saying they know. Once back to the Hakeem's apartment he pulls up to Marcus car, giving Marcus a handshake, saying he will get with him later, but now he is going to get his little girl.

Marcus smile saying he is going home and watch a seventies negro gangster movie with his family, Hakeem with word up! Marcus making it home taking a nap, and after his nap getting up taking a shower getting ready for the night.

About an hour or so, Stacy comes over, and Marcus introduces her to Grace. Grace giving Stacy a hug, then they go into the theater room in the basement where Jesse, Mellody, and Paige are Marcus introducing Stacy to Jesse and Mellody. Paige is like what's up girl, giving Stacy a handshake.

After watching the seventy superfly movie Jesse and Mellody goes upstairs, and Grace goes to her room. Paige starts to do a little cleaning while Marcus and Stacy talk. Stacy saying how impressive she is of this family, how close they all are, how the family can sit together and watch a movie.

Stacy smiling looking at Paige asking her do she needs any help, and Paige saying no, but thanks. Stacy whole Marcus by the hand going on to say she wish she and her sister were as close as he and Paige. Marcus with a smile ask Stacy why she is not close to her sister.

Stacy is like their father treats her different then he does her sister, Shelia, and if she can tell, she knows Shelia can tell. Stacy goes on to say she heard her parents discussing should they tell Shelia the truth that Ronald her father is not Shelia real father.

Paige stops cleaning, listening to Stacy talk, Marcus is like he is sorry to hear this. Stacy wipes her tears going on to say when their mother married her father, she was pregnant by some man in the military. She left that man not telling him she was pregnant by him to marring her father.

In the Meantime

Shelia is at work sitting in Kelly office before she goes on stage, Kelly never put pressure on Shelia because she is like family to her, but she knows something is wrong when Shelia wanting to sit in her office. Kelly ask Shelia what's on her mind, Shelia explaining the same she can't understand why her dad treat her different then her sister, and her mother have a hard time to keep eye contact with her, now teary eyes asking is it because she is a dancer.

Kelly knowing the situation saying them beautiful sandy brown eyes it's hard to keep contact. Kelley gets up giving Shelia a hug saying everything is going to be all right. Kelly goes on to say wipe them tears away and go out there and make that money. Shelia wipe her eyes getting up where she is sitting looking in the mirror saying how good she look, and she is going to make that money. Kelly saying well all right.

Chapter Five

A Dream

Paige laying in her bed thinking how good that ole school gangster movie she had watch with the family, now falling asleep, dreaming. Paige gets into a deep sleep and her dream takes on its own life. She and Stacy are sisters, and their mother name is Gloria, Goria the God mama.

Gloria became the God mama when she got the idea to follow in her father footstep and bootleg plus selling weed and she knew the right person to help her out was Lester. Lester was her late husband cousin.

Gloria, Paige, and Stacy got in her father's old truck, he left her and drove to the city to Lester's warehouse to get some liquor plus some weed. While at the warehouse Paige and Stacy loads the boxes of liquor sitting in the corner, while Gloria goes into Lester office to pay him for the liquor plus to ask him to spot her some weed to sell.

Lester like no problem he will have Marcus, his runner brings the weed to her by the end of the week. Gloria is like thanks for everything going on to say if anything was to ever happen to her will he look after the girls. Lester is like occurs he will.

Months later Gloria pass away from breast cancer never knowing she had anything wrong with her. After the death of Gloria, Stacy decided they have to figure out how to make some money. Paige with this mild look on her face asking Stacy not to worry, she got something figured out. Once she is in college, she is going to become friends with some of the smartest people who will be running the city one day. Stacy starts laughing asking but what does that has to do with anything now?

After hearing Stacy laughing at what she had just said, Paige still with this mild look on her face saying not to worry about anything how she has been saving most of her money. Paige going into her room and coming back with a suitcase opening it, showing Stacy how much money, she had saved.

Stacy starts to laugh the more, expressing this is the same suitcase their granddad gave their mom, and the same money. That when Paige starts laughing saying to Stacy, she is right, it is the same suitcase, plus most of the same money. Paige goes on to say she put more money into the suitcase. Stacy looking at the money in the suitcase expressing this is a lot of money.

Paige shouts, Yo, Sis, with this money plus the other money momma left them they are going to use all this money and turn it over to more money. Stacy asks how are they going to do that.

Paige answers, they know someone and that someone is Marcus who brought their mother her supplies. He keeps weed on him to sell, he got to be getting the weed from somewhere.

Stacy shouts, that's right, because when he come this way, he always wants to show how much money he has and asking them do they want to buy some weed.

Paige stresses, they are going to follow him to where he is getting his weed. Once they know who he is dealing with, they are going to go buy from that person, and start their business.

Stacy replied, 4-Sho! Paige expresses, once their mother died, she started planning all this, now she thinks it is time to execute. Stacy saying loudly, she is with her but also to say no matter what, looking at Paige, she is still going to college. Yes, Paige express, then saying she is going to one day become a lawyer like their mother would have wanted.

Paige and Stacy found out where Marcus hung out, they watch him until one day they follow him to this warehouse. Paige and Stacy realized this was the same place Gloria had brought them with her to pick up some liquor.

They felt okay because they thought Marcus was going to work, so Paige and Stacy got out of their car walking into the warehouse right behind Marcus. Marcus with this hostile look seeing them asking what are they doing following him. He then pulls out his pistol on them, Paige conveying wait, wait.

Before Marcus could say anything, Lester comes out with some of his guys, asking Marcus why do he have his pistol out. Marcus hollered, these little jive turkeys followed him here. Lester putting his hand on Marcus shoulder asking how did he let these little jive turkeys follow him here, Marcus saying nothing.

Lester then asks Marcus to give him his pistol, Marcus then put the pistol back into his pocket. Lester looks at Paige and Stacy expressing how sorry he was for the death of their mother. Lester now with a big smile, he yells Waz up! Giving them a handshake, then asking them what are they doing here.

Paige, like they are just trying to find out where Marcus gets his weed from, so they can buy some weed for their-self to sell. Lester smiling the more stating he can dig it, then asking what make them think Marcus is selling weed.

Stacy shouted when he brought their mother her supplies, he always tried to sell them some weed plus he kept a pocket full of money showing it off to them. Lester looks at Marcus asking is this for real, Marcus a little nervous mumble no, he has never tried to sell these little jive turkeys any weed.

Lester breathing hard saying, young blood! Then asking is he stealing from him. Marcus eyes open wide, saying no man, these little jive turkeys are lying. Lester with a smile expressing, young blood, he knows he has never gotten all of his profit back.

Lester then looks at Paige and Stacy asking them are they ready to manage some weight like their mother did for him. This surprised Paige and Stacy because they thought Gloria was just getting liquor from Lester.

Paige expressing 4-Sho! They are ready, Marcus hearing this yelling, what Lester. Lester looks at Marcus yelling back, to chill, be cool he still will have some weight to move. Lester going on to say but these two are like their mother, and he could rely on their mother. Marcus yells even louder, what Lester.

Lester takes a deep breath looking at Marcus saying he is not going to take too much more of this yelling. Marcus now nervous saying he is sorry. Lester is like that more like it, winking his eye at Paige and Stacy, then going on to say to Marcus what he does not know was these little jive turkeys daddy was his cousin, more like a brother to him and was his partner. So, God mama Gloria, she did not work for him, she had ownership now they have her ownership. Marcus uttered, these negros have ownership, these little jive turkeys are going take over his work and be above him.

Right on! Lester, with disappointment on his face yelling out to Marcus he was not smart enough to manage as much as he was letting him manage. Marcus huffing and puffing pulling out his pistol but before he could do anything, Lester's crew shot Marcus. Then Lester tell his crew to clean this mess up looking at Paige and Stacy conveying to them it look like they are in business.

Running Things

Two years later, everything was going good, and Lester loved how Paige and Stacy were managing themselves. He asks them if they can manage more work than they were already managing. Paige look at Lester, explaining she is headed to college, but Stacy shouted 4-Sho! Stacy now looking at Paige expressing they can manage all the work he wants to give them. Paige's eyes open wide with doubt while shaking her head at Stacy asking can she talk to her.

Lester seeing Paige's eyes open wide while shaking her head as if to say no way and hearing Paige asking Stacy to talk to her. Lester with a big smile saying go discuss this and just let him know because the work he is going to give the two of them will make both of them big time, plus big-time money. Stacy saying 4-Sho! They will let him know.

Paige and Stacy gets up and leaves Lester's office, and leaving the building getting into Paige's car. Once they are in the car, Paige asks Stacy is she sure they can manage more work because she will not be around.

Stacy smiling answering Paige, my sister she know she want be around, but this was always the plan she will handle the streets. Paige still with this concern look on her face saying my sister what's that got to do with them handling more than they are already handling.

Stacy smile the more conveying Mellody and Grace will have her back. Paige starts laughing saying those clowns, Mellody and Grace are crazy, yet both are like family very loyal and have always had their backs. Paige with Right on! Looking at Stacy, they get out of the car, and go back into Lester's office saying they can manage all he can give them.

Lester with, Right on! He knows they can because he liked how both of them went and discussed things, and that was how their mother would have done things. Lester, with laughter saying he would try to put more on her, but she would say she can only manage what she can manage.

Lester laughter turn to a little sadness expressing how Gloria was a great woman. Then Lester goes on to say while looking at Paige and Stacy before Paige go to college, he is going to teach them the whole operation, now looking just at Paige saying while she is in college he will be around until he feels Stacy can handle everything. Stacy responds with 4-Sho! She will learn everything and more.

Days Later

Stacy, she drove up into Mellody neighborhood, the hood, in her gold Cadillac Eldorado Coupe while Mellody brother sitting on the steps talking to his friends. Stacy gets her pick out looking in the rearview mirror and picking her Afro. Stacy then gets out of her car, with her bell bottom jeans, and platform shoes walking onto the steps saying Waz up gentlemen, then asking them which apartment does sister girl Mellody stay. Quinton with this curious look, turning down the music asking Stacy what do she wants with his sister, Mellody.

Negro Love

Stacy expresses that she just needs to talk to her about some business, if he can dig it, about that time Mellody comes out giving Stacy a handshake. Stacy then asks Mellody can they talk, as they walk out towards Stacy's car, Stacy having this meaningful look on her face expresses to Mellody. Yo! Sis, she has this proposition for her.

Mellody with excitement in her voice, she asks Stacy what is the proposition. Stacy saying she need her more now than ever before can she dig it! Stacy goes on to say be at warehouse tomorrow, around noon. Mellody said 4-Sho! After they finished talking Stacy gave Mellody a handshake.

Stacy gets into her ride driving to the pool hall hoping she can catch up with Grace there. Once at the pool hall Stacy goes inside, the first person she sees is Grace trying to hustle a dollar. Grace looks up seeing Stacy hollering Waz Up sister girl. Stacy responded that everything be all right sister girl, giving one another handshakes.

Stacy asks can they go somewhere and talk, Grace saying,

4-Sho, putting down her pool stick walking into the back of the pool hall. Grace now asking Waz Up. Stacy expressing her business is on another level now. Stacy with this serious look on her face going on to say to Grace she is going to take her from hustling in these pool halls and selling these nickel and dime bags, to selling wait kilos of cocaine, plus some heroin. Now with a smile Stacy asking Grace can she dig it.

Grace eyes are wide open saying 4-Sho! Stacy giving Grace a handshake then saying she has already talk with Mellody. Stacy expressing one other thing looking hard at Grace saying that crazy shit has to stop. Grace with her fingers cross relying 4-Sho! Stacy laughs, saying be at the warehouse at noon tomorrow.

That next day Mellody and Grace made it to the warehouse around the same time. Mellody sees Grace saying Waz Up! Mellody, saying it has been a long time, and Grace replies 4-Sho! It has been a while, both walks to the office and sees Stacy on the phone.

Once Stacy see Mellody and Grace, she replies she will be right with them. Stacy telling whomever she was conversating with over the phone she will get back with them, hanging up the phone. Stacy with a big smile looking at Mellody and Grace asking them are they ready to help her run the warehouse.

Both Grace and Mellody started laughing. Stacy starts to laugh with them, conveying she can dig it, about doing work in the warehouse but that is how weight is coming in and going out. Stacy laughter turns to seriousness saying this is big time know time for games.

Grace with 4-Sho! Mellody is like she can dig it, but all she knows is the hustle and the hassle of the streets. She does not know how to come to work. Stacy still with this serious look ask how much money they are making off them nickels and dime bags of weed they be selling on the street. Then Stacy laughs saying she will answer that not much, going on to say in a day here is months out there.

Grace saying okay she convince, she will do what it takes to make this work. Mellody is like 4-Sho! Stacy backing to smiling expressing that is what she is talking about. Then all of them getting up, Stacy giving both handshakes saying she will see them Monday, then going into her pocket pulling out some cash giving it to them saying go celebrate the rest of the week and be ready Monday.

After Stacy had gave them that money, Grace, and Mellody left the warehouse meeting at the strip club, buying drinks, and lap dances. After Grace and Mellody had been drinking, feeling fairly good they got to talking.

Mellody mumbled this warehouse thing more money, but the hassle of the streets is what she loves. Right on! Sis, the same here, Grace mumbling giving Mellody a handshake. Mellody ordering two more drinks then she goes on to say she have been staking out this small bank outside of the city and on Saturdays early in the morning there was never hardly anyone there at the bank.

Mellody smiling, she asks Grace would she like to help her do this job Saturday and they will have their own money to buy all the weed to sell on the streets. Grace with hell yes! Mellody replying Right on! Mellody going on to say there shouldn't be much to this job, they will be in and out within minutes.

Mellody and Grace toast to the bank robbery job for Saturday, turning up their drinks, Mellody then saying to Grace she will meet her at her place early Saturday morning, and they can drive her car because it is not registered in her name.

That Saturday morning Mellody and Grace met up getting into Mellody's car and while riding Grace pulls two guns out of her bag then she starts to load the two guns. Mellody looking over getting a little nervous seeing Grace loading them guns, but she did not want to let on, just smiling.

After driving for an hour making, it to the bank Grace hands Mellody a gun and a ski mask. Once in the bank Mellody hollering this is a hold up, everyone gets down, and do not touch that alarm, nor do anything dumb and everything will be okay.

Grace standing in front of the counter as the teller is giving her the money from all the registers. Grace and Mellody then ran out of the bank, getting into the car, and driving off.

Mellody asks how much they get, Grace saying a few hundred dollars. Grace now thinking Stacy had given each of them more money than that. About that time a county cop car is following them, and Grace gets her gun ready when Mellody saying chill be cool.

About that time the police car puts lights on them, Mellody pulls over. The police officer gets out of her car, coming up to Mellody's car, Mellody asks the police officer what the problem. The officer asking for license and registration, Mellody pulls out her license, and a bill of sale that she had made up on Friday.

Mellody explain to the officer she had just bought the car on Friday and haven't had a chance to register the car yet. She is going to do that first thing Monday morning, and the officer utter okay. Then the officer goes on to say, get that taillight fix it is broken, giving Mellody her license and the peace of paper back, the officer also saying have a nice day.

After the officer left, Mellody conveys that was close. Then Grace looking cross-eyed at Mellody asking her how she going to rob a bank driving a car with everything not working. About ten minutes later as they are driving not only is that police officer coming toward them with her lights on, but about four other police cars are coming toward them also. Mellody speeding up telling Grace to hang on, and about that time one of the police cars is upon them making them flip over.

That Monday morning Stacy getting a call from Paige asking her to turn on the news. Stacy, she turns on the news and the first thing she see is mug shots of Mellody and Grace. Paige shouting as Stacy is listening to her saying she should have left them clowns along.

It starts to thunder awakening Paige from her dream, she goes brush her teeth then goes to the kitchen where Mellody and Grace are sitting at the kitchen table drinking cups of coffee, and conversating. Paige laughs, Grace asks Paige what she was laughing about. Paige express nothing just a dream she had last night, then Mellody saying it must have been a good dream to remember to be laughing still.

Grace ask Paige was it about a boy, Paige looks at Mellody, then looks at Grace saying no she don't like boys, she likes girls. Mellody and Grace both looks at Paige saying they kind of knew that but wasn't sure, and glad now they know.

Paige now asking are they not upset, and Mellody comes over and give her a hug saying no, her happiness is what's important. Paige then ask what about her father, Mellody saying Jesse will feel the same way.

Chapter Six

Conversation

Paige is feeling real good since she let it out that she is gay. Then her thought of the dream she just had about being a drug deal, and Stacy was her sister. Paige now remember listening to Stacy converesation with Marcus after the movie was over. Paige looking at Mellody and Grace, now asking can she have a conversation about something she overheard Stacy talking about. Mellody and Grace putting down their cups of coffee both saying sure sweetheart. Paige take a seat at the table saying Stacy sister Shelia doesn't know her father is not her real father.

Paige teary eyes saying suppose she didn't know her father wasn't her real father how would she feel if she found out. Jesse walks into the kitchen the conversation stops and Paige gets up goes give Jesse a hug. Then Paige sit back down as Jesse pours him a cup of coffee sitting at the table. Paige goes on to say she would feel some type of way if it was her who is Stacy sister. Mellody ask who are Stacy parents, Paige saying she don't know.

In The Meantime

Early that morning things not going Shelia way a feeling of not belonging comes across her, as she leaves the club. Shelia thinking of what this older guy said to her while giving him a lap dance. The older guy repeated the same thing her father had said, she can be more than this.

Shelia starts to think how her father Ronald treats her with love, but he never treats her with the love he treats her sister Stacy with, his love for her seems to be at a distance. Shelia also thinking why her mother sometimes cannot look her straight in the eyes always looking away when they talk.

Shelia with tears starting to come down her face wiping each tear, and the more she wipes her tears the more tears. Now Shelia feeling this pain, this hurt she has never felt before coming upon her to where she can't take this hurt. She stops driving pulling over to the side of the highway trying to catch her breath. She then takes some deep breaths time after time breathing hard then pulls back onto the highway going home.

Shelia makes it home about six in the morning, she parks her car goes into her place and turn the air on low. She gets a glass of water goes to her bathroom looks into the bathroom cabinet and get her sleeping pills, going laying in her bed taking a hand full of sleeping pills drinking all her water putting the glass on her nightstand.

Aretha home asleep when this feeling wakes her giving her concern about Shelia looking at the clock seeing it's about six in the morning. Aretha knows something must be wrong because Shelia has never not call about this time saying she is on her way to get her daughter Zoie. Aretha with this feeling of scariness wondering why she have not received a call.

Bobby Shaw

Aretha with this scariness feeling coming upon her now thinking how she could have been a better mother to Shelia, compared to the kind of mother she is to Stacy. Aretha with a tear calls Shelia, but no answer then she calls once again, then time after time, still getting no answer making her worried.

Aretha wakes her husband Ronald telling him she is going over to Shelia to see if she is home. Aretha gets up putting on some garment, walking upstairs to Stacy's room seeing Zoie and Stacy are sleeping. Aretha goes back downstairs to the garage getting into her car opening the garage door pulling out of the garage driving over to Sheila. Aretha seeing Shelia's car in the apartment parking lot she calls Shelia once more still no answer. She then parks her car getting out and goes knocks on the door, but Shelia did not answer.

Aretha uses her key to go into Shelia's apartment calling Shelia's name. The coldness in the apartment giving her this chilling feeling as she walks to Shelia's bedroom seeing Shelia lying there with a pill bottle in her hand. Aretha hollers Shelia's name checking to see if she is breathing, checking her pulse seeing it is slightly low. She the calls 911.

While waiting for the paramedics Aretha being a nurse she turns Shelia's body face down, with the head turned one side and one knee bent. Aretha hearing the siren she gathers the sleeping pill bottom going open the door waving for the paramedics.

About that time Shelia threw up and when Aretha and the paramedics can into room. Aretha is so happy to see Shelia awake. The paramedics straps Shelia onto the stretcher taking her to the hospital in North Atlanta. Aretha gets in her car following the ambulance to the hospital. Once at the hospital where Aretha works, she reported that Shelia accidentally took to many sleeping pills. Once the doctor sees Shelia, seeing her heart rate is normal plus she is responding good, still the doctor explaining to Aretha Shelia is going to be admitted a day or two to be monitor.

After Shelia was in a room lying in her bed, and Aretha comes into the room, but before Aretha could say anything Shelia ask Aretha was she a mistake. Shelia now with tears going on to express to Aretha why she can't she look her in the eyes for long peroid of times as she is doing now, plus her father treats her different then he do Stacy. Aretha teary eyes looking at Shelia explaining to her she has the eyes of her father. Aretha taking a deep breath saying Ronald is not her biological father.

Shelia now in shock, and astonish as she can't believe what she just heard Aretha saying. Shelia wipe her tears away, now short of words looking at Aretha in confusion wishing all this was just a bad dream and she would wake up soon from this dream.

Back To The Conversation

About this time Marcus walks into the kitchen, Paige asks Marcus what's Stacy's parents name. Marcus saying Aretha and Ronald, Marcus then asks why. Mellody looking at everyone saying she think she knows Shelia and Stacy's mother.

Mellody goes on to say she remember when she first met Jesse, her friend Aretha a lieutenant nurse got pregnant by this one officer but married another officer, getting station somewhere else and she never saw her again.

Jesse's eyes open big saying he knows who the officer was looking at Grace but not saying anything. Grace looks at Jesse then asks was Sidney the officer and Jesse answered yes. Jesse goes on to say Sidney was dating Aretha, but she stops dating him and started dating this other officer.

Grace in shock as she listens to Mellody and Jessa. Jesse explaining Sidney never knew Aretha was pregnant, but he did hear the rumor about her being pregnant thinking the reason she married the other officer was because she got pregnant by him. Mellody is like she did not know the other officer was Sidney.

Marcus looking at Grace then he asks is what he is hearing true, Grace holds Marcus by the hand saying she do not know but hearing all this make her think it is possible. Marcus is like where did this conversation come from, everyone looks at Paige.

Paige looks at Marcus then expressing listening to all of this, she thinks Stacy's sister Shelia is his sister. Grace then saying she's not going to get into the know whether Shelia is Marcus sister, but she will support whatever he decides to find out.

Grace leaves the kitchen going to her bedroom sitting on her bed sadly thinking. Then she looks in her nightstand to read her book but instead she gets up goes to her closet and get a shoe box of a letter she had written Sidney, and his letter he had written back to her.

My Dearest Sidney

I know you have to do what you have to do thus, this makes you the man, you are my strong man, my hero, so I ask how are you my dear. I'm trying, wanting to be fair even though it's hard to be, yes, my dear this time I dreaded the most. I do not like having to feel this way, me not being with you, me not being able to be with the love of my life, how I feel so lonely, my dearest. How hard is this to know, I am here, and you are there, the distance calls makes you seem even farther away. I sit, I think while listening to your voice over the phone of us being together and to know I am separated from the one I adore, I cherish. How hard is this, I ask, I answer, extremely hard, I shout to the air damn, damn, damn!!! I love you, my dear

Grace

My Dearest Grace

As I awake this day, I awaken to the fact we are days physical detached from each other's love. Your hug I cannot receive, my hug I cannot give, your lips I cannot kiss, my kiss you cannot receive. Yes, these are hard days, how when I awaken, I reach for you, but you are not there how the distance has caused this. I think of how I miss the things we do, our love making is second to none, oh my! Have I miss our love making, but having you in my life gives me reason to hold on no matter what it takes or how difficult the situation is. I cannot imagine myself with another person, you are rare, your ways are pure, loving, and filled with utmost humility.

Sidney

Grace now teary eyes as she puts the letters back into the shoe box getting up putting the shoe box back into the closet going laying on the bed looking up at the ceiling asking why, why has this been put upon her, why had this to happen to Sidney, not to know he had a daughter he did not know, the loss of his life too young.

Back to the Hospital

Shelia so confused about hearing Ronald was not her biological father. Aretha holding Shelia's hand saying yes Ronald is not her biological father, and she must confess sometimes when looking her in the eyes-only seeing Sidney's eyes. Sidney's eyes were sandy brown.

Aretha take a moment than tells Shelia, her father's name was Sidney. How she did like him, but she did not love him. He was an officer where she was station at the time and when she met Ronald it was love at first sight. Ronald marring her because they wanted to be together, and he was getting station somewhere else.

Aretha with more tears looking Shelia straight in the eyes as Shelia also with tears hearing all that she is hearing. Aretha voice weaken while now explaining to Shelia when she was born how happy Ronald was. Aretha voice still weak but a smile saying he was so happy.

Shelia wiping her tears away with a smile thinking how happy her father was when she was born. Then her smile turns to sadness now knowing Ronald was not her biological father. Shelia then asks where is Sidney, and do he know about her. Aretha with sadness in her voice saying Sidney died years ago in a car accident.

Aretha crying now saying he never knew he had a daughter, and she is very sorry but when she decided to let him know, that's when she found out he had passed away. Shelia, with tears, looking at Aretha saying it is going to be all right asking can she come to stay with them until she can get her mind together. Aretha is like occur she would not have it any other way.

The next Day

Paige is standing at her car talking to Stacy about last weekend, the fun they had saying they got to do that again. While Hakeem waves at them as he is walking to his car. Marcus walk up to them asking Stacy can they talk about something on his mind about their conversation about her sister Shelia.

Stacy is like sure, but can it be tonight because she got to pick Zoie up from daycare. Marcus like okay as Stacy walks to her car, Paige and Marcus get into Paige's car and driving off. On the drive home Paige asking Marcus what is he going to say about Shelia. Marcus like honestly, he does not know, but he wants get to deep with Stacy about Shelia only more information.

That Night

Marcus calls Stacy about the conversation they had last Saturday about Shelia. Stacy is like yes, she should have kept that to herself, she does not know why she got so emotional. Marcus goes on to say to Stacy, Paige overheard their conversation talking to her parents and his mother about that conversation. Marcus pauses taking a deep breath saying how that conversation of Shelia got deep to the point he think he may be Shelia's brother.

Stacy asks Marcus why would he think that. Marcus explaining his Aunt Mellody and her mother Aretha were station together, plus good friends. Marcus goes on to say his aunt Mellody introduces his mother Grace to his father Sidney during that time finding out his father use to date Aretha before his mother. Stacy is like what, asking Marcus is he for real, then asking him can she call him back.

Getting off the phone Stacy calls Aretha asking her do she remember a lady name Mellody. Aretha saying nothing for a second then she ask Stacy where did she get the name Mellody. Stacy saying Marcus, his aunt is name Mellody. Aretha goes on to say she was good friends with a Mellody when she was in the military, but she lost contact with her over the years.

Aretha asks Stacy, Marcus aunt is Mellody, and they stay around the block from them. Aretha hype up going on to say to Stacy she must get Mellody number for her so they can catch up with things. Stacy express okay, but the reason she calls asking about Mellody is because Marcus thinks Shelia may be his sister. Aretha saying nothing for a second, then she asks Stacy how can that be possible.

Stacy with a little smartness in her voice saying she overheard some talking about her father not being Shelia real father. Aretha looks at Shelia as she lays in bed asleep, saying yes, Ronald is not Shelia real father, but what does that have to do with Marcus thinking he is Shelia's brother. Stacy then shouts because Marcus dad this man name Sidney who passed away years ago. Marcus aunt Mellody saying Shelia was his daughter.

Aretha saying to Stacy watch that tone young lady, and Stacy apologizes asking what is going on with their family. Aretha takes a deep breath saying tomorrow the family is going to sit down and talk about everything. Stacy now with laughter asking what about Shelia, Aretha still looking at Shelia as she sleeps saying she will be there. Stacy now laughing saying she can't wait to see this family sit down.

Getting off the phone with Stacy, Aretha calls Ronald expressing Shelia is coming to stay with them for a while. Ronald is like no problem, then Aretha explaining she told Shelia that he is not her biological father. Ronald like how did she take it, and Aretha replies they all need to have a sit down and discuss everything.

Aretha then saying Mellody lives in the same subdivision as they do, Ronald asks who is Mellody. Aretha with a little laughter replying she was station with her when they met. Ronald saying nothing at first then express oh yes! The big rump officer everyone was trying to get with, but not him.

Aretha with a yes, that's her, she lives here in the same neighborhood. Ronald saying great an old friend she seems to have been a nice person. Aretha express yes, but there is more to this than to see an old friend. Ronald is like what does that mean.

Arthea gets up from her chair walking into the hallway explaining to Ronald, Mellody's sister was married to Sidney, and that young man who took Stacy on a date is Sidney's son.

Ronald like what, a small world going on to ask Aretha where is she getting all this information from. Aretha with laughter replying their curious daughter Stacy. How she overheard them talking one day about Shelia, plus Marcus telling her about his family.

Ronald laugh saying Stacy she's in the know, and he wouldn't have it any other way. Ronald express he will fix a nice dinner. Aretha with a little laughter saying a dinner will be nice, but the sit down, and the conversation. Oh My! Ronald express yes, Oh My! Aretha then saying she loves him, and Ronald saying he loves her too, the both getting off the phone.

Bobby Shaw

Aretha going back into the room giving Shelia a kiss on the forehead, now sitting in her chair and she start reading a book.

Chapter Seven

Friendship

Frank is like dam, not knowing, but thinking Marcus is family. How he knows Marcus would be good in the game, more low key than Alfonso, more like him when as he was at his age, but he knows also his family would never forgive him if he let Marcus play or get in the game.

How his father Charles never talked to his father Oldman Perkin again once he and his brother David started bootlegging for his grandfather, but David had a plans, he was only doing it to save up for college to one day become a lawyer. Still Charles only going to his father funeral because his wife Sarah talked him into going, and also he never talk to Rosco again, and they were close, the best of friends, more like brother than cousin growing up together.

Rosco parents the undoable happen to them at Oldman Perkin club back in the day. This man was trying to talk to Rosco's mother, and his father did not like it, and got into it with the man. The man stab Rosco's father, and Rosco's mother saw his father being stab, she rushed the man, and the man stabbed her, both lying dead together. Afterward Oldman

Perkin shot the man, and killing him right there as he lay beside Rosco's parents.

Frank in his office going down memory lane thinking how he and his brother David got started working for his grandfather Old man Perkins at a young age, about the age of Marcus is now. Frank with a smile remembering how he use take them long rides with Rosco to Tennessee up in the mountains to get cases of moonshine for Old man Perkins. How always on the way back stopping right outside Atlanta in Fulton county dropping a few cases of moonshine off at this warehouse he now owns.

Those long rides how Rosco would talk to him about his son Jesse who he wishes he had gotten to know, and how his guilt of turning his back on Jesse he carried always with him. Frank remembering Rosco also saying if he ever got the chance to know his son he would support him in any kind of way, money or whatever.

Frank now thinking how he looked up to Rosco more than he did his father because Rosco would dress wearing suits like he was important. As for his father, he dressed like he was poor, just how he used to teased Sidney for how his father Lewis dressed.

Frank with a tear thinking how he loves his father. How his father wanting him to go back to high school and get his diploma, and if not his diploma, his GED. Frank with more tears thinking how he told his father in a smart way he is going to Atlanta to work for Rosco.

Frank with different tears now thinking how Rosco took the rap for him when he did the undoable shooting a man killing him when the man tried to rob them of the moonshine coming back from Tennessee at the warehouse. How Rosco got life in prison.

Frank shakes the thought of what happen during that time off, wiping his tears away, now back to thinking of the handshake he had gotten from Marcus. Thinking how much Marcus sandy brown eyes reminded him of his cousin Sidney. Thinking how strong Sidney handshake was, and now thinking how he uses to tease Sidney about his father being so country. How Sidney would chase him all over the farm but could never catch him.

Frank smiling then he calls David asking about when was the last time he talk to Sidney. David pauses then quickly utters Sidney has been dead for years. Frank pauses taking a moment then he wanting to ask David more, but David explaining he has a client coming in can they meet for lunch where they always meet.

Frank with sadness in his voice expressing meeting for lunch is a good idea. After getting off the Frank goes to his mini bar pours him a shot of cognac, taking the shot, and shouting this one is for Sidney rest in peace.

Lunch time in the city of Atlanta at this Rooftop restaurant.

Frank pulls up to the restaurant giving the valet the key to his new Mercedes-Benz G 63AMG, and about a few minutes later David pulls up giving the valet his key to his new Mercedes-Benz S 580.

Frank and David take the elevator to the rooftop to the restaurant sitting at the bar. Frank ordering two double shots of Cognac XO. Then both order stakes Frank well done and David medium well, while sipping on their drinks. David ask why now after all these years Sidney name comes up.

Frank is like he met this kid who has the same demeanor as Sidney, look like Sidney, and has Sidney's eyes, plus about the same size Sidney was at this kids age. Frank goes on to say the kid wants in the game. David is like first of all Alfonso is doing jail time and about to go to prison, David looking at Frank asking he want to bring another young man in the game.

Frank laugh saying Alfonso knows the warehouse, and the game in and out, but he got his mothers' attitude, he will figure his way out of going to prison. Frank going on to say no if Marcus is Sidney's son, then no. David express Sidney had a son who would be a senior in high school. About that time their steaks come out neither saying nothing else eating their steaks.

Afterward leaving the restaurant still on his mind Frank calls his mother, Sarah, asking about Sidney having a son. Sarah is like yes, Sidney's son Marcus, he and his mother came to visit years back, that is how the family found out Sidney died in a car trash.

Frank takes a deep breath saying to Sarah, he loves her getting off the phone. Frank pulls up to the warehouse parking in his spot. Frank, he gets out of his Mercedes-Benz G 63 AMG and goes to his offices. Kelly is in his office when he walks in. Kelly, she can see this look on Frank's face as if Frank had saw a ghost.

Kelly asking Frank what is wrong? Frank is like he cannot let Marcus get into the game. Kelly looks at Frank with this strange look then asking why, his age. Kelly getting a little anger in her voice, saying age it was not a problem letting Hakeem in the game.

Frank is like first calm down then saying it is not his age, but he thinks he is family. Kelly shouts Hakeem is her family, and Frank looks at her shouting, she let Hakeem in the game not him. Frank calms down going on to say if he let Marcus get involve the whole family will be down on him, and he do not need those problems.

Kelly is like what now, Hakeem has already got Marcus thinking he can play. Frank rants well Hakeem needs to getting Marcus thinking he cannot play, and he cannot be in this game. Kelly is like okay sweetheart getting up giving Frank a kiss on the jaw walking out of his office.

Kelly gets in her new Mercedes-Benz SL500, she texts Hakeem to come by the club once he gets out of school. Then Kelley, she drives off going to her place of business the Bin-Over a strip club. Hakeem seeing the text, texting Kelly back with okay.

After school Hakeem goes to the Bin-Over going into Kelly's office. Hakeem sits down asking Kelly what is up. Kelly expresses she is going to get straight to the point, Frank does not want Marcus in the game, Hakeem is like what, why.

Kelly then expressing there is nothing bad about Marcus. Frank thinks Marcus is a part of his family, and his family would not understand him putting Marcus in the game. Hakeem is like what! Marcus is related to Frank. Hakeem then he gets up saying he understand.

After Hakeem leaves the office Kelly, she receives a call from Aretha asking can they talk. Aretha and Kelly were best of friends in high school. Aretha paid her way through college striping with Kelly, but before Aretha can say anything. Kelly expresses that she understands she does not wanting Shelia stripping anymore. Aretha laughs expressing to Kelly, she knows her. Kelly saying yes, she knows her, and no problem.

Kelly always felt guilty letting Shelia come stay with her when she ran away from home, and not letting Aretha know but mostly the guilt Kelly felt was letting Shelia and Hakeem have sex and then having a baby, Zoie, afterward giving her a job stripping.

How Aretha was disappointed with Kelly, but once Zoie was born it did not matter how she felt about Kelly. It did not bother her Shelia started stripping because she strip at one time and Shelia was her on woman and the best she can do is to support her.

Hakeem leaving the Bin-Over getting in his car texting Marcus with can they meet up. Marcus texting him back with he will be off work at eight. Hakeem texts Marcus back with can he come by his place and Marcus with the text word up.

Around eight-thirty Marcus ringing Hakeem doorbell. Hakeem looking out of the peek-hole seeing it is Marcus opening the door giving him a handshake. Marcus walking into the place and Marcus is like what is up this must be especially important that it cannot wait until tomorrow at school.

Hakeem is like yes bro, asking Marcus to have a seat. Marcus and Hakeem having a seat and then Hakeem explaining he is going to get straight to the point going on to say to Marcus he cannot play, he cannot let him in the game.

Marcus is like what, why he do not understand asking Hakeem do he not trust him? Hakeem is like no, bro, he trusts him with his life. Marcus again asks then why, Hakeem saying because of Frank. Marcus ask because of Frank and then Marcus goes to say okay no problem but still Marcus was upset hollering dam, how he going to have the money to date Stacy.

Hakeem goes in his pocket giving Marcus two hundred dollars saying he know he going to do big things in life, and this is just a small investment plus when he needs more if he have it he will always be of help. Marcus is like no, he cannot take this money, nor any money later. Hakeem is like take the money, he insists, Marcus giving Hakeem a handshake saying thanks bro, then leaving.

Understanding

Paige and Marcus riding to school the next morning Paige asking Marcus why is he not saying anything. Marcus thinking why Frank does not want him in the game. Marcus utter he has a lot on his mind. Then Paige replies she understand, asking Marcus how did the conversation with Stacy go about Shelia.

Marcus utter they did not get to finish the conversation. Marcus smile at Paige saying he is proud of her telling his mom, and her mom the truth about her feelings about boys, and girls. Paige said thanks with a big smile.

During The Day

The doctor comes into the room looking over Shelia and giving her a good bill of health, then releasing her. Within thirty minutes the nurse comes into the room with a wheelchair taking Shelia to the lobby while Aretha goes and get her car. The ride home Aretha stops at Shelia's apartment to get her and Zoie some clothing plus other things they may need.

That evening Ronald had prepare dinner for the family knowing after the dinner the family is going to have a sit down. Aretha and Shelia coming into the house with Shelia and Zoie things. Shelia saying something smells good and about that time Zoie coming down the stairs seeing Shelia hollering

Mommie, Mommie as Shelia dropping her things and Zoie run into her arms.

Then Stacy comes into the room seeing Shelia holding Zoie taking Shelia clothing with Aretha taking Zoie clothing to Shelia's old room. Stacy and Aretha coming back downstairs. Ronald walking into the family room giving Shelia a hug saying dinner is ready. They all go to the dining room where Ronald had set everything up.

Shelia saying grace expressing this dinner she is grateful for and her father who prepare this meal amen. Then Aretha passing the food around as everyone is getting the portion they want, Aretha fixing Zoie's plate. Stacy takes a bit of her food saying this is good. Ronald had prepare his favorite dish stuff chicken breast with mozzarella and spaghetti sauce.

After dinner they all go to the family room, Shelia holding Zoie as they sit on the couch, Stacy sitting beside them, Ronald sitting in his favorite chair as did, and Aretha sitting in her favorite chair. Ronald began the conversation with how much he loves Shelia and going on to say, yes it's true he isn't her biological father but he's her father and there's not a day that goes by he doesn't think of her well-being, or how much he loves her.

Ronald teary eyes looking at Shelia uttering he is sorry if she thinks he treats her different than Stacy and if he did, he did not do it on purpose he love her, and she is his daughter. Shelia now teary eyes putting Zoie down getting up going giving Ronald a hug saying to him she loves him also.

Stacy looking at everyone mumbling, Sheila needs to know she has a brother. Shelia looks at Stacy saying a brother, yes, a brother Stacy said. Shelia looking at Ronald and Aretha. Ronald saying to Shelia he just found out the other day, and

Aretha conveying to Shelia saying Stacy knows more about her having a brother then she do.

Stacy looking at Shelia saying his name is Marcus. Stacy looking at Shelia the more noticing Shelia and Marcus having the same sandy brown eyes. Shelia asking Stacy who is this Marcus and how she know so much. Stacy explain he is her boyfriend, and his aunt knows their mother.

Stacy now looking at Aretha, and looking at Ronald saying to Shelia, Marcus aunt told him the situation of their mother with his father and how his father never knew he had a daughter. Shelia wanting to be mad but already understanding what Aretha had told her, she did not love her father. Shelia understanding, they were going to tell her, but Sidney had passed away in a car accident, and didn't see the reason to tell her, plus not to know Sidney had a son.

Shelia with a tear asks Stacy can she call Marcus and ask him to come by sometime so she can meet him. Stacy is like sure calling Marcus. Marcus answering his cell phone and Stacy expressing to him, Shelia wants to meet him. Marcus is like for real, asking Stacy when and Stacy saying now. Marcus with excitement in his voice saying yes, he is on his way.

Stacy and Marcus getting off the phone Stacy looking at Shelia telling her he is on his way. How this put a smile on Shelia face, Aretha and Ronald getting up from their favorite chairs saying to Shelia they are going to their bedroom to give her some private time with Marcus.

Ten minutes later Marcus is ringing the doorbell. Stacy goes and answer the door and when Stacy opens the door she could see Marcus seem nervous. Stacy looking at Marcus expressing to him everything is okay, Stacy and Marcus walk into the family room, then Marcus when he sees Shelia, and Zoie, he remembers when he brought her that money from Hakeem.

Shelia when she sees Marcus also surprise both hollering at the same time Hakeem, then Marcus gives Shelia a hug, then picking up Zoie saying his beautiful niece. Stacy telling Shelia she is going to take Zoie to her bedroom so she and Marcus can have some private time to talk. As Stacy and Zoie are walking out of the room, Zoie shouts to Marcus bye, bye Uncle Marcus.

This put a tear of joy in all theirs eyes, once Stacy and Zoie had left the room, Shelia asking Marcus to have a seat. Marcus sitting down on the couch and Shelia sitting beside him, both at the same time express they have the same sandy brown eyes. Marcus saying all his life he heard his sandy brown eyes are the eyes of his father and Shelia smiling saying she just heard that from her mother a few days ago.

Then Shelia asks Marcus how do he know Hakeem, Marcus smiling saying they are the best of friends. Then Marcus asks Shelia is Hakeem her boyfriend. Shelia stressing no they are just friend who had a baby together, but Hakeem is a good dad plus a caring person.

Marcus then with excitement saying to Shelia he wants to get to know her the more, how it feels good to have a sister, a niece and now that he know, he will always be there for them.

Shelia saying thanks, then going on to say, she is glad to have a brother, and she will always be there for him. Marcus getting up from the couch as is Shelia walking him to the door, Marcus giving Shelia a hug.

Shelia then asks Marcus for his cell phone so she can put her number in, Marcus giving her his phone. After Shelia puts her number in his phone then giving him his phone, waving goodbye shouting nice car. Marcus, he turns around walking back to Shelia saying he wants to share the car with her.

Shelia smiling asking Marcus why do he want to do that. Marcus expressing because their father had just bought the car the week he passed away. Marcus with a tear going on to say their father never got to drive the car and once he gets the money to buy him another car he is going to stop driving this car and save it in the memory of their father. Shelia is like thanks she is honor.

Marcus back at home Grace, Mellody, and Paige waiting up for him, Grace ask him how did everything go. Marcus with a smile saying everything went great. Marcus goes on to say he wants to know his sister and niece. Grace with a big smile expressing she is so happy for him, Mellody and Paige saying they are happy for him.

At the same time Aretha come into the family room seeing excitement on Shelia's face asking her how did everything go, Shelia is like great. Aretha give Shelia a hug saying how proud she is of her, for being so understandable. Shelia with laughter expressing to Aretha this whole conversation there has been eye contact, Aretha smile conveying there is no more guilt, the truth is out.

Chapter Eight

Back to Georgia

Laken, her passion for liberal arts, how she likes to entertain being the lead person in her high school play. The standing ovation of the audience how that done something to Laken's soul. Laken sitting in her bedroom thinking why is she wasting her time doing something she doesn't love, doesn't have passion for, she pulls out of her nightstand looking at something she had written.

Time is not to be taken for granted, does it stop to see what is going on, or does it tells the story from mourning when the sun rises with the light of the day from the east steadily moving across the land until sunset set in the west, with darkness of night turning back to the day of tomorrow.

Laken fills out an application online to get into Spellman the next fall. A month later she receives a letter from Spellman accepting her. That same day she calls Jesse and Mellody about staying with them. Laken telling them she has accepted into Spellman in their liberal arts program the next fall semester. Jesse and Mellody so proud of Laken getting into Spellman, and Laken with excitement wanting to get out of Chicago to get a feel of the south, she has never been anywhere.

Laken is very smart with a lot of talent. She wrote this when she applied to Spellman liberal arts program. Black and brown people matter, the black, the brown the silences of their voices, the ones with little money, with little respect, and yes look down upon never to be heard, for fear of putting unrest in the minds of others. What if given the opportunity the black, the brown, the invisible voices to speak how their circumstance was not ask for only given, and with opportunity their plans to achieve the dreams of success can be.

The thoughts of the black, the brown, the invisible voices to know to be successful will come with stress, sometimes with doubt, and sometime even with no appreciation, yet all the time with limitation, but with their success will reverse the situation of disrespect to respect, will give reason to escape the circumstance that was not ask to be given.

Excitement yet Not Excited

Laken after getting the okay with Jesse and Mellody to come to stay with them and seeing how close it's getting to Christmas. Laken wants to be in Georgia before Christmas having a conversation with Big Ben and Dororthy about driving her to Georgia.

Big Ben with excitement about Laken getting into Spellman, but more excited about driving his new Denali to Georgia. Dororthy with excitement about Laken getting into Spellman, but not excited about going to Georgia. This will be the first time Dororthy will have gone back to Georgia since she left years ago with Jesse's father Rosco.

Dororthy when she left Georgia coming to Chicago with Rosco she left her mother and father mad at them because they did not like nothing about Rosco. Dorothy back then with her afro, bellbottom jeans, and stack shoes on, remembering when she first came to Chicago on the bus with Rosco. How she had never seen that much heavy traffic in her life, plus the tall buildings with the Sears Tower in the background.

Rosco getting a job at this metal company in Chicago, how everything was going great. When Jesse was born and Dorothy wanting to go back to Georgia to visit her parents to show them Rosco was not what they thought of him.

That never came about because Rosco got fired, and after a few years of them struggling. Rosco left Dororthy and Jesse going back to Georgia bootlegging for his Uncle Old man Perkins. After Rosco left Dororthy, she met Big Ben who also work at the metal plant, and he stayed across the street from her.

Now

Big Ben with a big round stomach, and Dororthy is skinny as can be. Dororthy after thinking about it, her thoughts are she has nothing to be a shame of a successful son and a smart daughter who is going to Spelman. With a smile on her face now with excitement about going back to Georgia she calls Jesse saying they will be there two weeks before Christmas, and she want to introduce him to the rest of his family in Georgia for Christmas.

Jesse is like okay, then saying nothing just wondering about his family in Georgia because Dorothy never said anything to him growing up, and about having family in Georgia. Still Jesse is excited about Laken coming to stay and going to Spellman and knowing she will be a big influence on Paige about going to college. Also, Jesse is happy to know Dorothy and Big Ben is coming to visit for Christmas, plus a little excited to meet his family in Georgia.

Leaving Chicago

Big Ben drives out of the city traffic, and once he gets out of the city traffic on to the interstate to Memphis. Big Ben wanting to take the long route to Atlanta to enjoy all he can of his new Denali. Big Ben, he drives to the first exit and pulls over letting Dorothy drive the first few hours. Big Ben and Dorothy gets out of the SUV exchanging place, Dorothy setting the seat, and all the mirror, then she gets on the interstate.

Laken wants to put her headset on, but she forgot them hollering oh no! She has to listen to this music, this r&b from back when all the way to Atlanta. Dorothy favorite song comes on by Marvin Gaye, Let Us Get it On, Dorothy shaking her head as Big Ben is looking at her expressing last night when he needed some sexual healing she was to tired.

In The Meantime

Grace and Mellody are in the kitchen making some lemon pies when Jesse comes in the kitchen. Mellody asks Jesse to taste her pie which is still in the bowl, then to taste Grace pie which is still in Grace's bowl to see which taste the best. Mellody gives Jesse a spoon full of her pie bow. Jesse tasting the spoon smiling, saying this is unbelievably delicious. Then Grace giving him a spoon full of her pie bowl, Jesse with this look of oh my! Saying what is this.

Grace picks up a pie she had already made, and looking at Jesse, Jesse saying, no she will not, yes she will Mellody hollering. Jesse looking at Grace saying he was just playing, her pie is the delicious better than Mellody. Mellody pick up a pie putting it in Jesse face, as Jesse is wiping the pie out of his face, Grace takes the pie she has in her hand asking Mellody why did she do that to Jesse. Grace taking the pie she has in her hand putting the pie in Mellody face.

Mellody wiping her face as Grace starts running out of the kitchen, while Paige is walking into the kitchen, Grace runs into Paige, both falling to the floor. Mellody walks over Grace throwing a pie at Grace only to hit Paige. Paige wiping her face only to laugh, and Paige saying the children in this family. Mellody saying, she is sorry helping Paige up from the floor, and Jesse helps Grace up from floor. Marcus walks into the kitchen seeing the mess, and shaking his head only to say go clean up everyone, he will clean up this mess.

Atlanta

Big Ben the long route to Atlanta from Chicago via I-57 south to Memphis, via I-22 east to Birmingham via I-20 east, now right outside Atlanta seeing her beautiful skyline, then looking right seeing six flags, Dororthy her memory, her thoughts of Georgia she left as a young lady.

Big Ben, Dorothy, and Laken now at Jesse's gate calling him. Jesse buzzing them in, and once at the house Jesse waiting at the door with excitement walking out greeting them. Now they are in the house, and Mellody giving everyone a hug. Jesse introducing Grace and Marcus to Big Ben, Dorothy, and Laken.

Big Ben, Jesse, and Marcus goes to the Denali to get Big Ben, Dorothy, and Laken luggage, and taking all their luggage to the guest room, but taking Laken luggage to Paige's room where she will be staying until Big Ben and Dorothy leaves.

After a little conversation everyone settle in for the night. That next morning Grace and Mellody cooking breakfast for everyone, but everyone slept in Big Ben, Dorothy, and Laken was tired from the long drive. Jesse and Marcus eat some breakfast.

Negro Love

When Laken did wake up Paige asks her did she wants to go to a birthday party tonight in the neighborhood, saying it Marcus's girlfriend. Laken is like sure that sounds good, because knowing her mother she is going to be talking about growing up in Georgia, Paige laughs.

That night Laken, Marcus, and Paige leaves the house, while everyone else is sitting around in the theater room getting ready to watch an old movie called Mahogany. Before they start to watch the movie Jesse wants to know a little bit about his family before he meets them.

Dorothy expressing to tell them about the family it is going to take a while. Grace saying, they can watch Mahogany another time because she is not to up for a love story anyway. Jesse looking at Dorothy saying they have all the time she needs to tell about their family from Georgia. Jesse then asks what part of Georgia. Dorothy explaining between Dawson Georgia and Albany Georgia.

Grace express between Dawson Georgia, and Albany Georgia that's where Sidney family is from, then Dororthy saying Sidney, Lewis and Shirley has a son name Sidney. Grace getting teary eyes explain they had a son, he passed away years ago. Dorothy became teary eyes expressing she is sorry, she remembers how much Lewis and Shirley was proud of him.

Mellody and Jesse eyes open wide, Jesse saying wait a minute his best friend was his cousin wow! This put a tear on everyone's face, now Jesse asking Dorothy to tell them more. Dorothy wiping her eyes saying okay here is the story of their family.

In the Field

Dorothy starting with when she, Lewis, and Sarah was in the fields with their mother and father with hoes chopping the field. As their little sisters were standing in the field. How they all were barefooted, plus all of them with straw hats. How her dad Alvin and her brother Lewis in their overall, she, her mother Sallie, and her sister Sarah in some long flower dresses.

Dorothy smiling looking at everyone seeing how they all are interested in what she is saying. Dorothy shouts amen, saying her Father Alvin, when they were working the fields, how he would be singing spiritual songs and burst into tears. How they would run to him asking what is wrong, he would say nothing is wrong, simply happy, tears of joy, yes, tears of joy, tears to keep the soul clean.

Dorothy became teary eyes saying Alvin would say he has a strong family that he loves and is glad how they are surviving these challenging times. Dorothy wiping hers eyes now smiling saying wash days, her mother, and her sister Sarah how they would have them conversation.

Dorothy saying Sallie while she was washing, she would sing spiritual songs herself, and while singing, she would start shouting. They knew she was feeling the holy spirit, how she would shout amen and keep on washing all the garments they had to wash.

While Sarah would be helping their mother, she would do her sister's hair, which was a job within itself because Barbara, and Tina both had long thick hair. Dorothy saying after she finished doing their hair she would give Barbara and Tina books to read, while she would go to the tin shed to help with washing the garments.

Dorothy laughing the more saying how Sarah would get mad when she asks them what they had been talking about. Sallie would tell her everything she had already told Sarah.

Dorothy shaking her head saying but the hardest part was working in the fields. How hot it was in Georgia, working in the fields planting and picking crop, remembering the time how the thought of a drink of water was so refreshing. How them chicken running around the yard during the day, and that night becoming fried chicken for dinner.

The Next Day

Paige, and Laken sitting in Paige's room talking about how fun Stacy's birthday party was. Laken expresses Hakeem ask her can he take her out tonight, Laken goes on to say they are going to this Poetry Club. Paige laughing saying Hakeem is a senior in high school like she and Marcus is, plus he has a baby by Shelia, Marcus sister.

Laken laugh saying Hakeem might be a senior in high school, but he is the same age as she. Laken then asks Paige do not Marcus date Stacy, so how do they both have the same sister. Paige explaining Marcus and Shelia had the same father, and Stacy and Shelia have the same mother. Laken is like she understands.

That Evening

That evening Hakeem comes to take Laken out. Hakeem meeting everyone, and after Marcus introduces Hakeem to Grace he express he wish he had a mother as she. Grace asks Hakeem what is wrong with his mother. Hakeem pauses then explain his mother died when he was born. Grace and Mellody remembering the feeling of not having their mother.

Grace gives Hakeem a hug saying he can call her mother if he like. Hakeem saying thanks mom, and how not only did that put a smile on Grace and Marcus face it put a smile on everyone's face.

Big Ben utter young man take care of his daughter, and Dorothy express have fun. Hakeem and Laken left going to the Poetry House. Once there sitting at a table in the middle of the club. Laken looks around then she gets up as no one is on stage. Laken, she goes and ask the host can she speak. The host ask her name then goes to the microphone and introduce Laken.

Laken walks to the microphone she looks around the room then she looks at Hakeem and wink at him. Laken then she takes a deep breath speaking softly into the microphone, the words do you think, then she gets louder speaking, do you think you are going to get some of this beautiful chocolate body so quickly well think again, yet it is for the taking once my feelings can control my emotions of knowing. Knowing your feelings and emotions are in control, in control to know the truth of my dreams, my feelings for then I will not be afraid to let all this delicious chocolate go in the name of love, for then I will know your dreams, your feelings, I will know your love. The beauty of our love making will be because of patience, because of understanding, and the appreciation we will have for one another.

Laken stops speaking and she starts to drop the microphone, but she puts the microphone back on the stand as everyone starts to clapping. Laken goes back to her table, and Hakeem orders them two shots of tequila, after drinking his shot Hakeem, he gets up and goes to the host asking to speak. The host ask Hakeem his name then goes to the microphone and introduces Hakeem.

Negro Love

Hakeem takes the microphone looking around the room, looking at Laken winking at her. Hakeem then taking a deep breath smoothly saying on a ship in the middle of the sea, as the waves got so big, a shipwreck, now taking his last breath as the sea is drowning him. My last breath I thought, as a beautiful mermaid came and saved me, how she look at me, smiling while saving me, bringing me to shore, how she turn from a mermaid to this delicious chocolate young lady, how she change the way I think, my thoughts of what was love, only to know was lust, only to know what comes in the dark, only to leave in the dark, only in the light true love will come, for when true love comes I will understand myself the more, the better, my needs want be confused with my wants, my heart will have the freedom to say I love you, my thoughts will say you are the only one for me. Hakeem dropping the microphone as everyone stands up clapping, and this time Laken buys the shots of tequila.

Chapter Nine

Family

Jesse with grace, "Our Father, which are in Heaven, given us this day, our daily bread, this coming together of family, this coming together of love, we thank you for this meal that we are about to receive, amen." Everyone saying amen.

After dinner all the family are sitting around talking, Jesse asks Dorothy can she tell them more about their family. Dorothy smiles with yes she will be glad to tell more about the family. Dorothy gets up from where she was sitting, goes sits beside Jesse. Jesse, he put his arm around Dorothy.

Dorothy looking at everyone saying nothing as she was in thought, Dorothy now shaking as though it was cold in the house. The memories of back then Dorothy begin to say the cold winter in their house, how their mother would come into the family room yelling at Lewis, shouting if he does not get up and get some firewood from the shed, he is going to get a beating.

Dorothy smiling saying time after time Lewis at first would not respond, but when their mother would say do not let her wake their father. Lewis knew if their dad got woken, there would be hell to pay, and he really would get a beating.

Negro Love

So, Lewis would then jump from under the quilts to off the floor, uttering, okay mom, putting his shoes on and grabbing his coat. After Lewis had gotten the firewood into the house, Sarah and her would helped their mother fix breakfast.

Dorothy goes on to say they never would awake their dad until after breakfast was ready because. Dorothy with proudness' in her voice expressing their dad worked the land from the time he had breakfast to a few minutes for lunch, and back to the field to even, and something if the moon was bright. Their dad and Lewis would feed and water them mules and plow the ground over and over, until their mother would out come to the field saying enough for today.

During these times, he only asks for help after lunch from Lewis because he knew Lewis had gotten up early to keep the wood heaters going, but during harvest season, they all had to help getting the produce to the market.

Dorothy explaining she might be repeating some of her story, but her dad would come in for lunch every day, and after lunch, he and Lewis would work the land until they could not see anything but dark, and if the moon were shining bright he and Lewis would work even longer, until mother would say enough for the day. Dorothy with a big smile expressing how her father how so much he loved her mother, how what she said was the rule of the day.

Dorothy began to shake once more remembering them cold days, and colder night saying they had one little wood heaters, and two big case iron heaters to heat the house, plus for cooking. The house was four rooms, the kitchen, their Mom, and dad room, her, Sarah, Barbara, and Tina room, and Lewis slept in the family room on the floor.

Bobby Shaw

There was no indoor plumbing, an outhouse, the house was insulated with newspapers on the walls and plastic around the windows, the floors were wood, but the coldness coming from under the house. The house foundation was on bricks spread apart, and able to crawl under the house to play.

Dorothy shaking the more saying in the wintertime, the air came into the house under those floors, yet not in the family room. Their dad made sure that rugs covered all the flooring in the living room, he did not worry much about the other rooms because they were not going to be spending that much time in their rooms only to sleep.

When one of them would got sick or caught a cold, their mom would make the rest of them slept on the floor in the family room, getting their blankets, quilts, no one was to sleep on the couch. The one, or two who were sick would stay under the covers, and giving an old family remedy, which was corn liquor or whiskey mix with honey. Dorothy explaining their mother would make them drink that remedy until they would sweat the cold out of them.

Dorothy with a proud look on her face expressing their mother was smart how she negotiated with the landowners' wives to get the price she wanted for washing and ironing their garments. They liked her work, and they well respected her. How her mother took all that money she made and saved it, she had saved over ten years' worth of funds, never spending a dime.

Dorothy the prouder, the look on her face saying that is how their mother and father were able later to buy the farm because their father had a plan. He knew how honest the landowner was he was sharecropping for. He knew during that time many landowners were not that honest.

Dorothy going on to say their father, her brothers always planted a few more acres than the owner expected, and instead of taking that profit, they gave all that profit to the landowner. The landowner was always surprised.

Dorothy still with a proud look on her face explaining their father never asked the landowner for animals because he took the animals, the hogs, the chickens, and made sure they were reproducing before eating them. During that time, he took his old shotgun and did a lot of hunting, plus fishing, and just eating off the land, poke salad, and blackberries.

Perspective Memory Lane by Dorothy

Now owning their own land, people did not like it, but because of who sold the land to them, the landowner. He had a lot of money, owning the county they lived in, a lot of power in the state of Georgia, and no one wanted to go up against him. The landowner had a lot of respect for Alvin because if it were not for Alvin the landowner would have lost a lot.

Alvin made this landowner money sharecropping in the Great Depression when no one else was making nothing. The landowner had gotten incredibly old and knew when Alvin had the money to buy the land he had share crop, it was the right thing to do to sell it to him. The landowner told everyone in the county not to ever give Alvin nor his family any trouble.

The landowner sold the land to Alvin and Sallie because Sallie was his half-sister, the landowner's father was Sallie's father. No one knew at that time, but the landowner always had respect for Alvin and Sallie, plus made sure his wife also did, and everyone else.

Now Sallie and Alvin own their land, Alvin went back to the landowner and asked for a loan to build a better home for his family, and the landowner asked him was he sure he want to borrow money from him. The landowner said, come back in two days, and he will have some papers drawn up.

When Alvin, Sallie, and the children woke up the next morning, there was building material for the house everywhere, exterior red brick, siding, lumber, roofing, interior hardwood, sheetrock. When Alvin saw all this, he could not wait two days, he got into his old truck and went to see the landowner. When he got to the landowner's place, he said, there are many materials at his home, and he does not think he can afford to pay for all those materials.

The landowner with a big smile said, here is the contract, and when Alvin looks at the contract, he was in shock, the balance of the agreement was a dollar. Alvin shaking his head, asking, is this for real. The landowner saying yes, this is very for real. Then the landowner explains to Alvin asking him do he remember all that extra work above what they agree.

Alvin still in shock, the landowner said well after The Great Depression, he took that money and invested it in some mutual funds. How he has done well, plus he will never forget how he help him through the bad times. So, to show his thanks, the landowner said, pay him a dollar. Alvin reaches in his pocket with a smile on his face giving the landowner that dollar. When Alvin gets home, telling Sallie the story, how happy she and everyone was.

Alvin now using the money he was going to pay for the materials, gathering up all his friends that had the skills, and were out of work to help him build their new home.

How beautiful it is, the new house with hardwood floors, wallpaper on the walls, downstairs and upstairs, bigger bedrooms, a kitchen all can eat in at the same time, and the living room bigger than their whole other house, plus inside plumbing.

After the landowner had died, a letter came to Sallie, which confirm the rumor, the rumor was Sallie is his younger negro sister, and how their father loved her, but a shame to let her know, or anyone else. Once the landowner's father was on his dying bed, which the landowner was about twenty something years older than Sallie, his father gave a letter saying that negro girl that is here with her mother all the time while cleaning their house, that negro girl is family.

The landowner's father wrote, yes, his wife forgave him the day she held the baby. Even as much as she loved having a son, she always wanted a girl. So, she wanted the negro baby mother to keep cleaning their home so she could spend time with the baby, until her death. The letter went on to say from a distance love her, and from a far respect whoever she shall marry, for they may have a little of what he has been giving a lot of money.

Hanging Out

Dorothy and Sarah are at the Juke Joint, this guy trying to talk to Dorothy, but she isn't interested. He kept trying to speak then grab Dorothy's arm and said, let's go dance, and she said, no. Then Sarah grabs a pocketknife out of her bra and put it up to the chin of that guy, shouting, if he doesn't let her sister's arm go, she will cut his tongue out, now he letting go of her arm. The guy got so nervous when letting go, he trips and fell to the floor.

Sarah and Dorothy went to the other side of the room when Sarah meet Charles, and when Dororthy meet Rosco. Charles said, he saw what happen on the other side of the room, looking at Sarah going on to say she do not play, and Rosco looking at Dorothy asking can he get a dance. Dorothy with a smile saying yes, but Sarah looking at Charle hard asking do he have a problem. Charles putting his hands up making it clear no problem baby, no problem at all. Sarah looking the more at Charles expressing she is not his baby, she has a daddy. Charles smiling saying all right pretty lady.

When Charles said pretty lady this got Sarah attention, asking Charles do he thinks she is pretty. Charles quickly to say yes, gorgeous. About that time, Dorthy and Rosco came off the dance floor, and Lewis shows up from taking this girl Shirley home. Lewis expressing, they are running late. Dorothy with this look at Lewis like it his fault they are running late. Sarah saying if he was not messing around with that girl Shirley, they went be late.

Lewis, Dorothy, and Sarah going to the car, and Charles asks Sarah can he see her again. Sarah shouting, yes, she will see him here the next time they come. Sarah is about to get into the car, and there is a lot of noise, and Charles shouting asking when will she be back. Sarah shouting back, she do not know.

The good thing for Charles, he just had started working for his father, Old man Perkins who owns the juke joint, plus the grocery store on the negro side of town.

After making it home late that night, Alvin waiting in the front room for Lewis, Dorothy, and Sarah to come into the house. Once they are in the house Alvin with a look of disappointment and said, even though they are old enough to live independently. Alvin now shouting as long as they stay in this house they will not disrespected his rules by coming in here these kinds of hours.

Alvin then said his car is off-limits until further notice, looking at Lewis, and making it clear he needs to stop wasting his money drinking and start saving his money to get his own car. Alvin, now looking at Dorothy and Sarah, saying they need to start thinking of their future of finding a husband, instead of going to Juke Joint every chance they get.

Sarah said she might have met someone at that Juke Joint.

Alvin then asks, what does he do, and what is his name. The only answer Sarah could give him was Charles because that is all she knew. Then Alvin laugh, saying, well, he does not want her or Dorothy going to the Juke Joint any time soon.

Sarah asks, what about Lewis, Alvin said, what about Lewis, until he gets a car, if he goes anywhere, he will be walking. After Alvin left the room, Dorothy looks with this look of annoyance at Lewis. Dorothy then saying it is all his fault chasing that girl Shirley and leaving them there at the Juke Joint, and making them late getting home. Now Sarah is wondering would she ever get the chance to see Charles again.

Six months Later

Lewis, not wanting to disappoint his father, plus wanting to see Shirley saved every dollar until he had the money to put down on an old Ford coupe. Alvin was proud of what Lewis had done and gave him the rest of the cash to get the coupe.

Lewis also remembers how he had gotten Dorothy and Sarah in trouble that night six months ago. Lewis asking them do they want to take the first ride with him. Dorothy and Sarah both said yes wanting to get away from the house. Dorothy and Sarah jump in the car, and Lewis drove them around.

Lewis saying, he is thirsty, and stopping at the colored store so he can get a drink. Lewis pulls up to the store getting out of the car. Lewis asking Dorothy and Sarah are they getting out, both said, no, but saying bring them back something to drink too.

Bobby Shaw

Once Charles is in the store going to the cooler to gets some drinks, and he notices this guy mopping a spot in the store. Lewis now thinking, how do he know this guy, so he goes up to the guy. Charles stops mopping asking Lewis how is his sister, tell her he's been thinking of her.

Lewis responds, come with him, and tell her himself because she is outside in the car. Lewis pays for the sodas, then he and Charles goes out to the car, Sarah looks up with a smile hollering Charles. Sarah, with excitement, gets out of the car giving Charles a hug saying she has been thinking of him. Charles with a bigger smile expressing he has been thinking of her.

Charles going on to say, not knowing if he would ever get the chance to see her again. How he waited at the Juke Joint for the last six months hoping she would come back. Sarah asking Charles is this where he works. Charles answering, yes, here and the Juke Joint, his father owns both. Sarah saying okay, they live out in the country, and their dad has a farm. Charles said he thinks he knows where she is talking about.

Lewis said, they got to go, Charles again hugs Sarah, Sarah getting in the car and as they rode off, Charles looking, and waving, as is Sarah waving out of the car window.

Once they arrive home Sarah jumps out of the car and runs up to Alvin kissing him on the cheek, and Alvin asks what is that for. Sarah said just because she loves him. Sarah then saying remember all those questions he had asked her about the guy she met at the Juke Joint. Sarah laughing saying well she got the answers.

Alvin thinking, he does not remember that conversation, and now asking what questions. Sarah said when she told him she had met someone at the Juke Joint. Alvin still don't remember but saying okay. Sarah smiling the more explaining she met him again today, and she have the answer to the questions he asked months ago.

Sarah said, his name is Charles, and his father owns the Juke Joint, plus the grocery store on the colored part of town. Alvin with yes, he knows the owner, Old man Perkin, he is a good man. Alvin looks at Dorothy asking her when is she going to meet some she likes.

With a smile on Dorothy's face, she starts laughing, saying when he let them go back to the Juke Joint. Alvin said, well, Lewis has a car now—Alvin walking away smiling and shaking his head.

Alvin goes into the house loudly calling Sallie's name, Sallie running down the hallway, asking what is wrong. Alvin saying nothing is wrong he just wants to tell her something. Sallie takes a deep breath saying do not scare her like that calling her name for nothing so loudly. Alvin gives Sallie a kiss on the cheek, going on to say he is sorry, but he excited about Sarah meeting Old man Perkins, son.

Sallie said the bootlegger, who own the Juke Joint, Sallie laugh saying she remembering when they use to go to that place. How Old man Perkins use to give them free drinks, and now their daughter likes his son. Alvin said, yes, when she talks about him, she lights up. Sallie said she needs to speak with Sarah to see where her head is she do not want any grandbabies just yet.

When Sarah comes into the house, Sallie with a smile on her face making it clear this boy that got her nose all up in the air, she is not ready for no grandbabies. Sarah smiling looking at Sallie expressing she do like him, he is very nice, plus he thinks she is pretty. Sarah giving Sallie a kiss on the cheek saying she ain't ready for no children, skipping out of the room.

Chapter Ten

Christmas Week

Barbara and Tina every year always rode together from Atlanta to Albany, and stopping in Dawson picking up Sarah going to their parents' farm between Dawson and Albany Georgia.

Once there at Alvin and Sallies's home they always trying to help Sallie and Shirley with the baking of the cakes, and as always Sallie would say never mind she and Shirley got this. Sallie knew none of her daughter had baking skill, but Dorothy and she haven't saw nor heard from her since she left with Rosco years ago.

Barbara, Tina, and Sarah they would then start decorating a little of the house, and never in no hurry knowing as always they come to stay the hold week before Christmas staying in their old rooms as when they were growing up.

How during the week, they are putting up lights all around the house waiting for their husband to bring the Christmas tree, laying out all the Christmas ornaments, and rapping gift. The house smell of baking, and pine scent, making it feel of the holiday spirit.

Bobby Shaw

After about three days in Jim, and Larry would meet Charles and Lewis on the farm going getting a Christmas tree. This day after they had gotten the tree bringing it in the house this new Denali shows up, and Lewis walking out on the porch trying to see who it was. This big man first gets out Lewis not knowing who he was. Then Dorothy gets out, and Lewis seeing her, runs off the porch to her. Dorothy running toward him teary eyes each giving one another a big hug.

Dorothy introduces Big Ben to Lewis going into the house, Sarah, Barbara, and Tina dropping everything they were doing with their hands over their mouth going up to Dorothy hugging on her, and Shirley hearing all the noise coming to the family room, from the kitchen seeing Dorothy now teary eyes, giving Dorothy a hug.

Alvin coming in the family room as is Sallie. When Alvin sees Dororthy for the first time in years saying finally he has been looking for her all day, and glad she was okay. The guilt Dororthy felt at that moment saying yes, daddy she is okay. Sallie saying nothing just holding Dororthy's hand tightly not wanting to let go.

Everyone else introduces themselves, then Lewis asking Dorothy and Big Ben where is their luggage. Dorothy saying they are going to get a room in Dawson, and everyone at the same time saying nonsense. Lewis, looking at Big Ben, Jim, and Larry saying let get their luggage. Shirley smiling looking at Dorothy saying her room is still the same as the day she left, every week she dust the room.

Dorothy lost for words teary eyes sitting beside Sallie and Alvin. Alvin wiping the tears from Dorothy face asking her what is wrong asking her did that boy Rosco hurt her, and Sallie is just holding her hand tightly. About that time Lewis, Big

Ben, Charles, Jim, and Larry comes back into the house taking Dorothy and Big Ben luggage to Dorothy's old room.

Sallie and Alvin getting up from sitting beside Dorothy saying they are going to bed. Sallie giving Dorothy a kiss and Alvin saying to Dorothy after a long day he is glad she showed up. Dorothy hugs Sallie tightly and hugs Alvin even tighter.

Once Sallie and Alvin left they finished decorating the tree, and then Barbara hollering it is egg nogg time, and Dorothy ask egg nogg time. Sarah saying yes, this is what they do each year drink egg nogg and Uncle Nearest whiskey and be merry. Tina grabbing Dorothy by the hand as they all go to the kitchen.

Shirley passing out glasses, and Barbara getting some Uncle Newest out of her pocketbook while Sarah getting the egg nogg out of the refrigerator. Barbara putting the Uncle Nearest whiskey on the table, as did Sarah putting the egg nogg on the table. Everybody fixing them some egg nogg and whiskey.

Lewis, and the fellows when they came back down the stairs. Lewis shouted man cave, everyone but Big Ben knew what he was talking about. Lewis has half the barn built into his man cave, with big screen TVs, hardwood floors, heat, and air, plus a bar with some of the best moonshine money could buy.

They go to the burn, once in the burn Big Ben is awe-struck, Lewis man cave is just as nice as the family room is in the house. Lewis getting some glasses from behind the bar, some peach, and strawberry moonshine putting all this on the bar saying pour up them trouble.

Big Ben pouring him some peach moonshine then after drinking that moonshine asking Lewis can he try some of the strawberry moonshine. Lewis looking at Big Ben saying bro!

Yes, drink it up, and Jim holler toast to family. Larry raising his glass saying toast to family, and they all turn up.

Sallie and Alvin are in their room, and Sallie looking at Alvin shaking her head. Alvin smiling expressing she has been gone for years, and he just want her to feel a little guilt. Alvin goes on to say he will let her know he got the memory of an elephant before she leave. Alvin giving Sallie a kiss then saying it good to see her. How he has miss her, and Sallie agreeing with yes, it good to see her, and she have miss her too.

After a few drinks Dorothy going to her room seeing everything is left where she left it, when she left, her favorite doll, the first negro doll made. Dorothy remembering when she got that doll when she was a little girl, and remembering Alvin building her doll a rocketing chair, and she sitting the doll in the rocketing chair where the doll is sitting now. Dorothy picking up the doll she called Ebony holding her saying she is sorry.

The emotion going through Dorothy, Big Ben coming into the room feeling a little woozy saying they should have been to visit. Dorothy lays in Big Ben arms now crying saying he is right she have a beautiful family and should have never turn her back on them. Big Ben express he needs some sexual healing, lets get it on, Dorothy kiss him turning the other way in the bed saying not to night.

Christmas Eve

The rest of the family coming a little at time, Jesse, Mellody, Grace getting rooms for them Paige, Laken, Shelia, Zoie, and Marcus, Marcus having his own room, at TownePlace. As did David, as did Frank and Kelly getting rooms at TownePlace for Christmas eve.

Yes, Christmas day, Saturday! All the family on the farm Dorothy introducing Jesse, Mellody, and Paige to the family. Lewis and Shirley are surprised to see Grace and Marcus, but more surprise when Lewis see Shelia saying who is this young lady looking like a younger version of Shirley. Marcus saying Shelia she is his sister, and their granddaughter.

Lewis and Shirley with joy on their face hollering Sidney has a daughter. Marcus expressing yes, and he just found out himself. Shirley looking at Shelia, then hugging her tightly, and Lewis asking who is this beautiful little girl. Zoie, holler she is Zoie, and Shelia saying this is her daughter. Which this brought even more joy to Lewis and Shirley saying they are so happy, what a Christmas gift.

As The Day Goes On

Shelia now teary eyes, Lewis, Shirley asking her what's wrong, and Shelia saying, she is happy to be with her newly met family, her grandmother, grandfather, great grandfather, and great grandmother. Shelia goes on to say the success of this family. She wishes she had.

Barbara asks Shelia why don't she feel she cannot be successful. Shelia takes a deep breath saying because she is a dancer. Everyone starts to laughing, and Lewis looking at Barbara and Tina saying they dance, but look at them now owning their own law firm. Tina then expressing thanks to the education from Spellman.

Laken eyes opened wide looking at Tina and Barbara saying she will be going to Spellman next semester. Barbara saying that's great, and Tina give Laken a hug.

Now R&B is playing all over the house, when the song by Shalamar, "Second Time Around" comes on. Grace is in the kitchen with Shirley trying to be of help. David has been checking out Grace understanding she was married to Sidney, but he did not want to be disrespectful, but there is something about Grace he cannot help himself, but wanting to get to know her.

The reason Grace is trying to be of help is because she has an attraction for David hearing he is single, but she also did not want to disrespect the family. Grace thinking to herself, thinking this longlines, this place where she is, is this meant to be, or by choice. David walks into the kitchen, Shirley can tell there is an attraction, and she wouldn't have it any other way if the two of them connect.

Shirley walks out of the kitchen saying she will give them some along time. After Shirley left Grace asks David why is he single a successful man as himself. David with a smile explaining the reason he is single was because he always approached women who thought they were all that and a bag of chips.

Grace then asks David can he not have a good relationship with women who has confidence. David smiles the more saying no, women with confidence are women who are needed, but this one woman, she thought she was all that and a bag of chips. David pauses saying Vanessa, and going to say he had fallen in love with her, yet he lost his love for her because she was only about her feelings. Grace with wow, asking David do he still want to be with this Vanessa.

David looking at Grace in a way that he has found his queen, now shaking his head as to say no. Then he expresses she has no place in his hearth, his eyes are on what is going right now, and right now at this moment. David goes on to say to Grace let not her heart be suspicious of him, he would never do anything to deceive her, nor try to hurt her. David takes a deep breath saying he would never pretend to care for her, nor would not he never pretend to love her. Grace with a big smile hearing David expressing himself. Grace then gives David a hug walking out of the kitchen.

In The Meantime

Lewis, Jesse, Frank, and the rest of the fellows are in Lewis man cave drinking moonshine watching a basketball game, Jesse and Frank were the only two in the room pulling for this player to get a tribble-double, everyone else in the room did not like this player who left a team he was on only to go to a team making a super team.

Once this player got that tribble-double, Jesse and Frank toast becoming friends, once Frank realize Jesse is Roso son. Frank wants to be a closer friend to Jesse, remembering how Roso was good to him, and remembering Roso telling him his only regret was not to get to know his son.

About that time David comes to the man cave, and Frank ask where has he been expressing he miss a good game. David express so, but he found something better Grace. Jesse smiling expressing Grace was married to Sidney, how he and Sidney were the best of friend.

David listening to Jesses with concernment which turn to a smile once Jesse saying Sidney would be happy to know Grace has found someone good, winking his eye at David, and then David gives Jesse a handshake.

Frank pouring Jesse and David a shot of Cognac XO he had in his suit jacket saying toast to family and new family. Alvin seeing them drinking Cognac XO saying enough of this moonshine asking Frank for a shot of the Cognac XO. Frank saying sure granddad pouring him a shot. Alvin drinking the shot saying oh my! This is the best shot in all his years of drinking, putting his glass out saying give him another shot.

In The House

Sallies has the attention of all the ladies of the family, telling a story about a child name Love. How the child got this name from his mother, it was not his real name, but she called him that all her life to the point that is what everyone called him Love.

Over the years Love became very wealthy, very respected in the community everyone wanted Love around. They value what he had to give, he knocked at ones doors, and they would answer it because Love gave help to all that wanted. Love was okay with those people asking him for what they wanted, and he did not mind giving them their wants.

Sallie pauses looking in the eyes of all the lady now holding Zoie. Sallie goes on to say Love never realized he never knocked at the doors of the ones that needed his help. The day came Love became very sick, and when he went to his doctor, his doctor examine him, and afterward his doctor saying there's nothing she can do.

The doctor told Love if he would like a second opinion, do so. Love utter, okay he will. That next day Love knew this other doctor he trusted and got a second opinion, and that doctor saying the same thing there is nothing he can do. How brokenhearted Love was to hear that.

That night when Love had made it home as sick as he was feeling, he went straight to bed, but at first, he could not sleep because of the tears coming down his face. The more he wipes the tears away the more they came, but at last, the tears stop, and he then went to sleep.

As he was sleeping an angle came to him asking him why the tears. The angle goes on to ask do he have more than most people, yes, Love mumble. The angle ask once again then why the tears. Love explaining because he don't have long to live, and once he die, he don't know where he will go. The angle utter, oh my! Love then saying he gave to the ones who wanted, but he do not know if that was enough, nothing else said the angle left.

The next morning Love awaken by the feel of the coolness of the morning jumping up feeling great but realizing he had been sleeping under a cardboard box. Love look down seeing a note saying for who has the most, the most was expected than the ones who have the less. Go knock on these doors today, Love looking at the number of doors saying there is no way. Love had started to move, and there was another note saying just knock at this one door.

This lady looking in her cabinet seeing only one can of tuna, and nothing more, not knowing how this one can of tuna is going to feed her two little children. She got down on her knees saying God let his will be so that she may feed her children she is not worried for herself.

A knock at the door, a little boy answer the door seeing who it was shouting Mr. Love, Mr. Love. Love asking to come in as the little boy runs to his mother bedroom, but she was coming out of the kitchen seeing Love standing at the door. The lady ask Mr. Love to come in, Mr. Love walks into the house saying his life is over, and he have much, giving the lady a check for a million dollars saying he hope this meets her and her family's needs.

Bobby Shaw

The lady eyes wide open not believing what is just happening, but saying thanks, and Love saying it is his pleasure as the lady walks Mr. Love to the door she looks to the heavens saying thank, as did Love looking to the heavens smiling, and feeling good about what he just done.

Sallie saying the end of this story, but something to consider think about what is the good that needs to be done, who is going to be Mr. Love in trying times, not only in good times. Sallie kissing Zoie saying this family is bless.

Sallie express one more thing she knows the good, the bad, the tension of some in this family. Sallie with a big smile expressing the magic of this family is praying, a praying family no matter who think they are right, and think other in the family are wrong, pray, pray, pray!!! There are many hearts, many ideas in this family, but praying is what is always in common.

Sallie smiling the more, still holding on to Zoie, saying she know everyone wants to get to that egg nogg and Uncle Newest whiskey, and she do too. Sallie going on to say always be of an open mind, an open heart of family, of friends making friends feels like family, embrace the power of that love, be easy to forgive with the heart, and hard to hold on with the mind. Sallie shouts egg nogg time.

Chapter Eleven

Church - Free

Free the preacher saying at five o'clock in the morning the day after Christmas, Sallie, Alvin, Shirley, Lewis, Sarah, Charles, Big Ben, and Dorothy sitting on the front pew. How free are the ones spending more time judging others yet wanting to be free. How free are the ones wonder how others got to where they are yet will not put the time to get there themselves. How free are the ones running from who they are to what others want them to be?

Yes, free the preacher is saying standing at the pulpit, the ones who understand to be free is not to stay worried, but to have faith even in the worst of time. The preacher now filling the holy spirit his voice is getting louder preaching yes, free are the ones understanding freedom comes with a price, but with praying and faith that price is paid.

The congregation saying amen, the preacher walking from the pulpit, now jumping up and down, and wiping his sweat with his handkerchief. The preacher preaching let the heart be free to see the beauty of ones needs, having enough faith to stay attainable, letting go of pride, letting go of insecurity, for the door of truth has open to see how to be free.

Bobby Shaw

The preacher asking the congregation can he get a amen. The church saying amen! The preacher going on preaching use hesitation to let the bad pass by, catching a ride with the good. Let not wants overtake the mind, nor let not pride consume the heart, for to be free is to know your needs are justified and your wants are sometimes because of pride.

The preacher stops jumping up and down calmly walking to the pulpit saying he was afraid of his ability, never to give himself a chance, yet some way, some-how confidence show up and saw the capability in him, which set him free, only God, only God, amen!!!

The preacher saying Oh My! How can one be free covering up their suffering with an act pretending to be okay, not letting go and letting God. Be free the preacher saying, let go and let God, understanding the satisfaction of knowing God is fighting the battle.

The preacher saying one last thing before he go, knowing it's early on a Sunday morning and some may be hungry, free is love an unconditional love that spills into the heart, with the passion of loving the things about us despite our mistakes, refuses to let go of the happiness it has for our well-being, trying to find something in our faith beyond the imagination, to keep us where we need to be, not pretending to be happy with us when we do wrong, but always loving us no matter what goes on. The preacher asking for a amen, the congregation saying amen.

Church adjourns for the morning service, Shirley, Sarah, and Dorothy goes and help with breakfast for the morning service. The preacher seeing Dorothy for the first time since he saw her in the Juke Joint back in the day, remembering he wanted to dance with her, but she did not want to dance with him. The preacher with a smile remembering Sarah pulling the knife on him, which over the years, he and Sarah laughs about back then. Dorothy smiling but didn't know what to say, only to say beautiful sermon. The preacher shaking her hand saying he is glad she came to morning service.

Church - Feelings

Barbara, Jim, Tina, and Larry come sitting on the second pew behind Alvin, Sallie, Dorothy, Big Ben, Shirley, Lewis, Sarah, and Charles, for the Eight o'clock service. The preacher saying amen! Standing at the pulpit, saying a bless morning pausing then asking the congregation do he have their attention, the church saying amen!

The preacher starts speaking, at one time in his life he was listening to something that was getting close to him, and what was getting close to him was called doubt. The preacher saying, he started asking himself why is this coming upon him, asking himself is there something he done, or doing, or just how he thinks of himself.

The preacher saying amen, saying doubt had him right where doubt wanted him to be, but the Holy Spirit came to him with the feeling of getting him where he needed to be. The preacher pausing then saying from this feeling of a low place in the mind, and suffering in the heart.

The preacher starting to get some loudness in his voice preaching when he felt what the Holy Spirit was giving him now he was able to let within come without turning his negative thoughts his unbalance of life into positive thoughts. Yes, the preacher shouting his life became balance, balance giving thoughts of love, the protector of the mind, and yes, food for the soul with a piece of mind knowing doubt can only stay if we let it stay.

They preacher preaching the Holy Spirit is always there, but it needs to be awaken, awaken by praying, praying every thought, every minute, no matter whatever else is going on inside the mind, inside the heart, no matter what the day may bring. The preacher voice calms down saying pray then wait, wait for the sensation of the Holy Spirit putting upon the heart the stimulation, upon the mind, a reason to love self, a reason not to doubt self, a reason to know this will not be for a season, but an everlasting time.

The Preacher preaching pray for other, pray when they go the bed at night with a heavy load of doubt on their heart, they can awaken with the Holy Spirit on them, for there is nothing God cannot do, the preacher asking for a amen! The church shouting with amen.

The preaching standing at the pulpit saying he leave the church with this, trust in God, trust in God with all the might the body can stand. Seek the strength from above, the faith to use his love, learning his will to live. To be loved in a way that flaws does not judge, but only judge by the gratefulness of the heart.

Church - Love

David, Frank, Kelley, Jesse, Mellody, and Grace sitting on the third pews behind the rest of the family. Hakeem, Laken, Paige, Marcus, Sheila, and Zoie, all sitting on the back pews.

The eleven o'clock service, the preacher standing at pulpit asking the church for an amen, the church saying amen. The preacher asking the church do they know how love feels, not the boyfriend, girlfriend kind of love, but the love of God.

The preacher she pauses, looking around the congregation then she reply she met that kind of love when it came knocking at her door. The day she and her children had little to eat, lights were about to get cut off, and she had no one to turn to, just to get on her knees praying, and that day the mailman came knocking on her door, asking her to sign for this certified letter.

The preacher she is now getting louder walking from the pulpit preaching when she opens the letter it was a check, a back time child support check in the amount of seven thousand dollars. The preacher shouting, yes, God's love answering prayers, try him, try him with all ones faith, and then wait and see. The preacher, preaching God's love will put a smile on your face, pep in your step, and yes, happiness in your heart, try him, try him with all ones faith.

The preacher asking for an amen, the congregation shouting amen, then the preacher walking back to the pulpit saying she will leave the church with this. Know that God's love us all, there is nothing he do not know about each and every one of us all he wants for us all to come to him, call on him, have faith in him, and he will solve all our problem. Yes, we have to have faith, trust in him and once we ask him have no doubt in him, just let go, and let God work it out. Amen!!!

After service everyone fellowshipping going to the church cafeteria, the senior pastor of the church blessing the food. The sister of the church had made fried chicken, pork roast, potato salad, mac & cheese, green bean casserole, sweet potato casserole, greens, cornbread, caramel cakes, pound cakes, sweet potato pies, and pecan pies.

Shirley looking at Sallie and saying she is going to fix Alvin and Lewis plates, and she will be back for next service. Shelia hearing Shirley asking can she help fixing them plates. Shirley saying sure sweetheart, putting a big smile on her face.

Church - Crossroads

The evening service, Shirley made it back, and the rest of the family still there, the preacher praying grateful, grateful in the name of Jesus. Speak to them Jesus, speak to their souls, to their hearts, and let them know the battle is not theirs. The family hearing the preacher saying, troubled, stress out, driving those problems down the road of life, yes, driving those problems down the road of life not knowing which way to go, lost, yes, lost not knowing to turn right, to left, or keep the same path. Oh My! The preacher preaching the Holy Spirit can come upon us asking to drive, yes, asking to drive us down the road of life, yes, to have faith in God letting him do the driving letting go, and letting God.

The Holy Spirit now has the preacher as he is jumping around, with a handkerchief in one hand, wiping the sweat from his face, and the bible in the other hand. The preacher shouting, let go and let God, there will be no decision at the crossroads of life, pain no longer, them tears of sadness will turn to tears of joy, letting God fight them battles.

The preacher asking for an amen. The Holy Spirit all over the church, as the church is hollering amen, while clapping. The pastor calms down walking back to the pulpit saying open them eyes to see the miracles of God and listen with them ears to hear the words of God. Even when the rain comes the love of God is still there, no storm comes that God do not know about, have faith in him. Amen!!!

The preacher praying, work with our hearts so that we may know how to understand to live right together, learning to forgive is away to live, knowing to love comes from above, letting the world know that you have put us all here together, and no one can take us apart, but us Amen!!!

Back Home

Once back home Frank felt so good about today's services, but still not about the things he has done in his life. He has these feelings coming over him, these feelings of guilt. Everyone follows everyone back to the farm, Frank gets out of his car looking up to the heavens with everyone in the yard, shouting please forgive him of his transgression in life. Everybody was a shock hearing Frank say that, but saying amen.

Dorothy teary eyes thinking of her crossroad of life how she had to prove a point keeping her from her family. As the family walks into the house, Dorothy holding Sallie's hand, as they walk into the family room. Dorothy looking at Alvin still while holding Sallie's hand now crying saying she is sorry, and she so sorry for turning her back on the family.

Alvin gets up from where he was sitting, and goes over wiping the tears from Dorothy's face looking at her, saying she did not turn her back on the family giving her a hug. Alvin going on to say just don't let it take this long again. Dorothy shouts once or twice a year for now on. Alvin saying one other thing there's nothing wrong with him, or his memory he got the memory of an elephant. This made Dorothy so happy now hugging Alvin.

Chapter Twelve

New Beginning

Vanessa frustrated with the relationship she is in spending the Christmas holidays along not being able to get in touch with her boyfriend, now having trust issues.

The ride to work after the holidays, a Monday morning, Vanessa listening to some old school r&b on the radio when the song "Everything" come on, bringing tears to her. Vanessa thinking how she made a mistake leaving David for who now is her boyfriend.

Vanessa now at her station working beside Grace when Vanessa asks Grace why is she so cheerful, that glow, where is this coming from. Grace smiling saying during the Christmas holidays she wore red meeting this wonderful man.

Vanessa is like that is nice looking at Grace with a big smile expressing she deserves all the happiness she can find. Vanessa going on to ask Grace to tell her more about this wonderful man she met. Grace is like he is a genuinely nice person, and attractive.

Vanessa is like no, no, she wants to know what he does, plus what is his name. Grace with a big smile saying his name is

David, and he is a lawyer. Vanessa big smile turns to disappointment. Grace seeing the disappointing look on Vanessa's face now in thought thinking is this the Vanessa David was talking about.

Grace then asks Vanessa did she use to date David. Vanessa saying nothing for a second or two, and then she asks Grace why would she ask her if she dated David. Grace looking at Vanessa still with a smile saying, first when she said David that smile of hers went away, and second David told her that a Vanessa broke his heart leaving him for someone else.

Vanessa is like yes, she made a big mistake, looking at Grace now with a smile expressing David is a good man, and she is happy for her. Grace gets up from her chair giving Vanessa a hug saying thanks.

Vanessa leaving her station going to give a patient some medication, now in her thoughts, thinking this uppity (B), got the man she should be with. Vanessa thinking, she needs to get a grip, as she walks into the patient room this beautiful older lady probably in her early ninety.

Vanessa give the older lady her medication, as the older lady can feel the unbalance in Vanessa spirit. The older lady sharing what is not to be, and ain't mint to be. The older lady smiling, as Vanessa asking the older lady if she needs anything.

The older lady saying the only thing she needs is for the time to come that she will meet her maker, for then she will have happiness, the happiness she lost while making wild choices, choices with no future of love, choices to think what was love was a lie, and now only to be along.

As Vanessa leaves the room her heart drop thinking she doesn't want to die along, and she doesn't want to be an old lady along in a hospital room. Vanessa goes back to her station seeing the glow on Grace's face back in thought if only that glow was hers.

She asked herself, what has she done leaving a good man she knows she would have had a future of love, and only now to hope the man she is with will give her that future of love. Grace seeing Vanessa in thought asking her is she alright. Vanessa saying occurs she is all right.

Then Vanessa uttering no, she is not alright her patient just told her she is waiting to meet her maker, for then she will have happiness. Grace looks at Vanessa saying she can actually understand what was said by the patient, for she felt that way for a long time never to know if she would lose that feeling, that feeling of not being happy.

Now the guilt Vanessa is feeling thinking what her thoughts of Grace were, knowing Grace is a nurturing person, there is nothing to think bad about her, there is no mystery of her.

As The Year Went On

Grace is her room reading and thinking of David when Marcus comes to her room knocking on the door. Grace saying come in Marcus walking into the room with a big smile showing Grace his tuxedos for the prom. How Grace looks at Marcus saying she is proud of him then giving him a kiss on the cheek. Marcus smiling saying he is proud of her to be dating and enjoying her life.

Prom Time

It's day's before prom at Marcus and Paige's school, and Paige needs a date to the dance. She didn't know whom to ask, so she spoke to Marcus about it. Marcus expressing to Paige to relax as he knows the right person to ask is Kim.

Paige express Kim, Marcus saying yes, she is fun to be around, always beating him and Hakeen in basketball. Paige asking Marcus if he think she will go with her. Marcus place a call to Kim explaining to her how Paige doesn't have a date to the prom, and if she is willing to go with her. Kim saying yes, Marcus giving his phone to Paige, Kim and Paige exchange numbers. Once off the phone Paige with this big smile looking at Marcus saying thanks.

The next day since prom dates was settled, Paige calls Stacy to go with her shopping for a prom dress and accessories. Finally, shopping was done, Paige picked out beautiful and well-colored dress, matching accessories.

Prom Day

Prom day arrives as Hakeem, Kim, Stacy arrives over Paige's home at the same time, Hakeen in a nice dark blue suit, Kim in this nice grave tuxs, and Stacy in this beautiful light blue dress. All speaking walking to the door ringing the door bell. Grace, Mellody, and Jesse taking picture of Paige, Laken, and Marcus when the door bell rings. Jesse going and answering the door seeing Kim, Stacy, and Hakeen asking them to come in to the house.

Grace looking at Marcus seeing how much he looks like Sidney, and she gets teary eyed, she realizes how much of a man he is becoming. She's feeling emotional about everything now joking saying to Stacy to take care of her son. Stacy replies with a smile she will take care of him, and she will return him home in one piece. About that time the limo arrives, and they all go get in the limo.

Prom Night, awards are given to certain individuals who rock their senior year to its fullest impact. The time comes for the awards, and silence fills the halls. Nominees and winners for the various categories are call.

Hakeem isn't left out in the male category. He was given the awards of Best Dress, Most Sophisticated, and Most Influential male. This was a shock to Hakeem because he didn't even know he was nominated.

The crowning of Prom Queen and King, speculations were made as to whom would emerge winners finally, it is announce, Marcus and Stacy are Prom King and Queen, and as they take the stage this is accompany with much screams as Paige and Kim are hollaring Marcus and Stacy's names.

Stacy, so loved and she had a lasting pleasant impression on people, but she never knew it was this intense until now how she is teary-eyed hearing speech, speech. After being crown Prom Queen Stacy walks up to the microphone, and she began to speak expressing she was taught first by her parents to live and give love freely without restrictions, yet in bad time restriction may disapear, but still life goes on, and she certain will try and make the world a better place.

Relationship

David and Jesse have become close cousins, David call Jesse asking can he meet him at Lenox Square at Mayors Jewelers. Jesse asking David when. David saying an hour or so. Jesse saying no problem, and getting off the phone. Jesse goes to Mellody saying he is going to meet David, and he think he is going to buy a ring and ask Grace to marry him. Mellody looks at Jesse asking him why do he think that Jesse kissing Mellody on the jaw saying David want him to meet him at Lenox Square at Mayors Jewelers.

Negro Love

After Jesse met David at Mayors Jewelers, David asks Jesse do he like the ring he picking out showing him a two-carrot solitaire ring. Jesse saying yes, expressing Grace, she will really like this ring. David then buys the ring. When Jesse makes it back home, Mellody seeing the big smile on Jesse's face, Mellody now smiling asking Jesse, and Jesse saying yes, he bought her a two-carrot solitaire ring. Jesse goes on to say he will be over here tomorrow morning right before lunch to take out Grace.

The next morning how the sound of the birds singing, everything seems inharmony, and with a nice morning breeze. Grace sitting on the patio reading the book she had only got to a certain page, and stop, but now she is well passed that page. Mellody comes out of the house having a seat on the swing, looking at Grace saying she finally finishing reading that book she gave her, Grace saying nothing.

Mellody laughs seeing Grace is into the book, so she gets up goes back into the house. As the morning goes on, Mellody comes back out on the patio giving Grace a glass of lemon aid, asking her is she coming into the house because it is getting a little hot out here. Grace with a smile saying, yes, it is getting a little hot out here, but she just wants to sit out here a little longer, so she can get her mind together.

Grace liking David a lot, but she still feels a little guilty of him being Sidney's cousin. Mellody asks Grace what is on her mind. Grace saying, David and Sidney. Mellody express she is going to be straight with her. Mellody takes a sip of her lemonade, then taking a deep breath saying, move on, plus it's too hot out here to be thinking about what's gone forever, knowing what's here now. Grace looks at Mellody saying she is right, both getting up going into the house.

Once in the house Jesse and David sitting at the table drinking a cup of coffee. Once Grace sees David she cannot help but to have a smile on her face. David gets up from where he is sitting giving Grace a hug, then asking her is she get ready to go. Grace asking ready to go, David express yes, asking her do she remember their lunch date.

Grace looks at David saying she is sorry she totally forgot. Grace ask David can he give her a few to change into something nice, David smiling saying occur, sitting back down while Grace change into something nice.

Grace comes back out with a nice sundress on, David looking at her saying she looks genuinely nice, and then David asking Grace where would she like to go for lunch. Grace saying anywhere will be all right, David with okay taking her this soul food restaurant.

After lunch on their ride home, listening to some old school on the radio when the song, "Come Share My Love" comes on, Grace asks David if he thinks he will settle down. David smiling saying, yes, once he can meet and get to know that special lady. Grace laugh looking at David saying well, she is a special lady. David expresses that he knows, and he do not want to waste to much more time.

David stopping the car pulling over on the side of the road going into his pocket getting the two-carrot solitaire ring out asking Grace to marries him. Grace teary eyes holding her hands to her mouth, then saying yes, yes, yes she will marry him. David put the ring on her finger. Grace giving David as kiss. David pulls back on the road driving home.

Once home Grace and David walking into the family room, Marcus, Paige, Mellody, and Jesse are waiting on them to come in. Marcus gets up and give David a handshake, then giving

Grace a hug. Mellody and Paige are so excited after seeing the ring Paige hugging Grace. Now Mellody teary eyes and just the happiness being share.

Monday

Monday morning Vanessa riding to working listening to this old school radio station thinking how bad her weekend went, the loneliness feeling even with her boyfriend there beside her the whole time. This song comes on, "Yearning For Your Love" and the thought of David crosses her mind.

Vanessa goes to her workstation and the first thing she sees is that two-carrot solitaire ring, the glow on Grace's face, how the hurt Vanessa is feeling, but saying beautiful ring. Grace smiling saying thank, then saying she and David got engaged this weekend. Vanessa expresses she is so happy for her, but the pain made her walk out of the station thinking if she calls and tell David she made a big mistake he will take her back. Vanessa goes into the lobby and calls David.

David recognizes the number but did not answer. Instead, he calls Grace saying Vanessa just tried to call him. About that time Vanessa walks back into the workstation. Now Grace looking at Vanessa cross eyes, but not saying anything. Grace's thought is she know how to manage a two-face snake.

The Plan

David and Grace double dating with Jesse and Mellody, and when Mellody ask when will the wedding be, David looking at Grace, and Grace saying they are going to the courthouse as soon as they can get some free time. Mellody shaking her head saying no the hell not, come on now, not the courthouse.

Mellody smiling goes on to ask what about something small at their beach home facing the ocean, the location its beautiful, and privacy. David with a big smile looking at Grace saying that will be a great idea. Grace holding David hand tightly asking when. Mellody express what about a month from now because that will be before the kids go to college, everyone saying okay.

The Wedding

David giving the minister something to read, David with his white two-piece linen suit on, standing under a conch shell and areca palm fronds with florist fresh cut arrange into the aisle, and leading up to bamboo arch decorated with flowers. The sound of the ocean the wave back and forward everyone sitting, Frank, Kelly and Hakeen sitting on one side while Jesse, Mellody, Paige, and Laken are on the other side. Marcus with this nice suit on, and Grace with this white sexy extravagant dress. Marcus hands Grace a bouquet while walking on the beach to the location of the wedding.

The minister standing right outside the bamboo arch, as Marcus and Grace approach with music playing here comes the bride, and Marcus escorting Grace down the aisle. Marcus giving Grace a hug whispering he love her going having a seat. Grace now standing under the arch on the left side of David.

Negro Love

The minister asks who gives this bride away. Marcus raising his hand as to say he do. The minister reads what David had given him. These feelings of mine I have never felt this honest with anyone. Now I can tell my feelings, trust to talk to you about anything and get a genuine opinion about everything. These feelings to pull up out of me the sense of hope, the emotion of happiness, and just the feeling of belonging was deep within me lost, now found.

The minister finished reading what David had given him, and the minister looking at David asking him do he take Grace to be his wife. David with a smile saying, he do, then the minister looking at Grace asking her do she take David to be her husband. Grace with a smile saying, she do.

The minister then ask is there anyone with any objection, nothing but silent, the minister, he now pronounce the two of them husband and wife. The minister looking at David saying he may kiss the bride. David kissing Grace then they jump the broom.

Champagne after the ceremony as they celebrate the beginning of a new life together for David and Grace. David and Grace taking photos under the arch. All the family taking photos, after taking photos there is a wedding cake delivered to the beach home.

The family and the minister goes to beach home for the reception. Grace cutting the cake feeding David a piece. Then Mellody cutting the cake giving everyone else a piece. After everything was over, everyone goes back to the Hotel, packing their luggage preparing to drive back home.

Grace back at her room packing when David knock on the door saying he chartered a yacht to take them out on the ocean for their honeymoon. Grace hugging David. After everybody had packed their things, now in the Hotel's lobby, everybody giving pleasantries, saying goodbye.

David and Grace drive to the chartered yacht. Once on the yacht, Grace and David are so in amazement. The Capitan introducing the crew, the first mate, the engineer, the deckhand, the stewardess, and the chef.

As the yacht is taking off, David and Grace goes to change into something more comforting. While changing, David looks at Grace, expressing how much he loves her. Grace comes closer to David giving him a kiss saying she loves him as they are kissing, David takes Grace by the hand laying on the bed making enthusiastic love.

Afterward David and Grace shower putting on what they came to change in, they go on the deck as the stewardess bring them their meal. The chef had prepared some BBQ chicken and a pasta salad, a nice selection of alcoholic. Both choosing a glass of red wine.

After the meal David and Grace sipping on their glasses of wine the view of being on the ocean at night is so beautiful. David holding Grace's hand as they are sitting on the deck of the yacht looking at the night sky. They see a waxing crescent moon so bright now tinkling stars in the shape of a heart, as a shooting star runs in the middle of the stars as though cupid is shooting an arrow through the heart.

Grace look at David, they kiss, both made a wish to themselves, and how both wishes the same thing love and happiness. David looking at Grace with excitement in his eyes thinking his heart is in a place of amazement as is Grace thinking the same thing, her heart is in an amazing place.

Chapter Thirteen

Gambling

Jesse was gamble once more when basketball playoff began, not thinking what would happen if Mellody was to find out. How he placed a bet winning a few hundred dollars, but by the time of championship game Jesse had lost thirty thousand dollars.

After the championship game the next morning Jesse was sitting in the family room along thinking his marriage is over. Jesse knew he could not cover this up and when Mellody finds out. Jesse remembering that disappointing look she had on her face the last time this happen.

Jesse shouting dam, dam, dam!!! Thinking how he promised Mellody he would never gamble again. About that time, he gets a call from Frank asking him was he still riding with him to see Rosco. Jesse like occurs, thinking he is going to see his father for the first time would take this off his mind. Frank saying he is in route and will be there depending on Saturday morning traffic in about fifteen minutes, and Jesse saying he will be waiting.

When Frank pulls up in the gated community the gate was open, and Frank pulls his Mercedes-Benz G 63AMG to Jesse's house. Jesse walks out the house as fast as he could getting in Frank vehicle saying he has never been in something so nice, so luxury. Frank with a smile saying thanks, and then expressing to Jesse Rosco is going to be so happy.

As they are riding every mile or so Frank would start coughing, and Jesse asking Frank was he all right. Frank was like he keep a dry throw, taking a peppermint. Jesse thinking nothing else of it, yet needing to talk to someone about how he was feeling about losing all that money, plus now knowing he will lose his wife. Jesse broke down with a tear telling Frank he going to lose his wife, Frank looking at Jesse with concern asking why. Jesse wipes his tear away telling Frank because he lost a lot of money gambling, and he promise his wife he would never gamble again.

Frank listening, thinking how good Rosco was to him, he asks Jesse how much he lose, Jesse utter he is to embarrasses to say. Frank reply they are family do not be embarrassed, and Jesses mumble he lost thirty thousand dollars, and Frank saying nothing else on the ride.

When they got to Macon Georgia, Frank stops at a bank he has account with, and telling Jesse he needs to transfer some money he will be right out. Jesse thinking nothing, but a little nervous because this would be the first time he would had saw his father since a child.

Frank coming back out of the bank giving Jesse an envelope expressing to him to save his marriage. Jesse looks inside the envelope and there was thirty thousand dollars, Jesse expressing he can't take this amount of money, and Frank acknowledge Rosco gave him a lot more money than this.

Frank with a smile expressing this vehicle he is driving and his business he owns was because of Rosco. Frank expressing it is an honor to help family in need with a stressful situation. When Frank express he would be of honor, Jesse remembered Sidney saying the same thing when he asked Sidney to be his best man.

Jesse saying thanks, then he shouted thanks, giving Frank a handshake, Frank with no problem asking Jesse is he ready to meet his father. Jesse taking a deep breath saying yes leaving the parking lot of the bank, but once they got to the prison it was on lock down, no visitor. Jesse disappointed and Frank express they can come another time, Jesse is like for sure.

That Evening

Mellody asking how was everything. Jesse, with this disappointed look, looking at Mellody explaining the place was on lock down, and he did not get to see his father. Mellody gives Jesse a hug saying it will be another time. Then Jesse gives Mellody a kiss thinking how Frank saved his marriage.

They now sitting on the couch beside one another Mellody looking at Jesse with a smile on her face thinking how much he has kept his word, and not gambling anymore. Jesses looking at Mellody with this feeling of gratitude, how from this morning to now he has a better perspective on things that are meaningful, never again to take anything for granted, and what is meaningless, gambling to let it go.

In The Meantime

Shelia feeling lonely not dancing anymore, not getting that attention, but she does not want to go back down that road. Shelia thinking how her new founded family is giving her support, yet still there was an emptiness, a void of love missing.

Shelia goes lay down beside Zoie as Zoie is sleeping, the warmth in her heart that comes to her from looking at her beautiful daughter. While she was laying there looking at the ceiling her cell phone rings, and Shelia answers it when a voice she cannot recall saying he got her number from Hakeem, he is his cousin. Shelia saying oh yea, asking him his name, and he saying Justice. Shelia express yes, she remember him when she stayed with Vanessa, and he and his sister came to visit.

Justice saying word up, Justice going on to say he do not mean no disrespect, but he been thinking about her all these years. This put a smile on Shelia's face because when she saw him she was attractive to him. Justice explaining the reason he was approaching her now was because when he finally got the nervous to talk to Hakeem, and Hakeem gave his blessing.

Shelia expressing with a little laughter Hakeem gave his blessing, he is special, but his blessing was not needed, although he is a good person, and they are very much alike, and the only good came from them was Zoie. Justice ask can he get to know her and Zoie, Shelia feeling her void leaving, asking Justice can he give her time to think on it, Justice saying take all the time she need.

Shelia saying it want take that long asking him to call her tomorrow night, Justice with excitement saying he will do. They getting off the phone, Shelia calls Hakeem, Hakeem express he was just going to call her to let her know he gave his cousin Justice her number. Shelia expressing, he just call, and Hakeem saying he is sorry because he was not supposed to call until he got the okay.

Shelia with a little laughter saying that is okay this time. Hakeem with a little laughter saying thanks, going on to ask how is Zoie, plus do she need anything. Shelia saying she is sleeping right here beside her, but she is going to need to some money herself because she not dancing no longer. Hakeem express he heard, no problem he will give her whatever she needs. Shelia saying five hundred will do for now.

Hakeem is like okay, he will give it to her tomorrow. Hakeem goes on and ask Shelia is she going to keep her apartment. Shelia replies yes, her Aunt Barbara, and Aunt Tina gave her a job being a receptionist at the firm, plus they are going to pay for her to become a paralegal. Hakeem expressing that is great, and he will take care of the bills until she get situated.

Shelia saying okay thanks, going on to say once she gets on her feet, all she needs him to do is to take care of his daughter. Hakeem with a little pep in his voice saying she is always going to be taking care of and she come first. Shelia express even with a new lady friend, Hakeem express Zoie is always first, getting off the phone.

The next day Shelia and Zoie meet up with Hakeem that evening, at his place when Zoie coming into Hakeem's place she runs straight to the refrigerator grabbing her an ice cream sandwich. Hakeem handing Shelia the money. Shelia saying thanks, and telling Zoie to give Hakeem a hug. Zoie giving Hakeem a hug saying to him she loves him, Hakeem saying he loves her too, then Shelia, and Zoie leaves.

That night Justice calls Shelia asking her how was her day. Shelia saying great, asking Justice how was his, and Justice saying he spent his day thinking of her, Justice going on to say it was great.

After conversating for about an hour Justice ask can they go out this Friday. Shelia laugh saying she have not been out on a Friday in a while. Justice ask why is that. Shelia pauses and saying she use to dance on Friday and the weekends. Shelia asking Justice is there going to be a problem of her use to dancing, Justice laughs asking is there going to be a problem him selling drugs.

Shelia expressing to Justice she do not have no problem with what he do, as long as he do not bring it around her child. Justice explaining he will never do that, and he has no problem if she was still dancing. Shelia with a little laughter saying yes, Friday will be nice, and giving Justice the address to her home.

Friday comes Justice picking up Shelia calling her from the gate, Shelia letting Justice in and when he made it to her house she gave Zoie a kiss telling her to be good with Stacy. Shelia goes to Justice car saying she is not ready to introduce him to anyone. Justice smiles saying he understand.

Justice ask Shelia where would she like to go, Shelia express anywhere nice asking Justice do he like jazz and Justice saying yes, taking her to St. Peter Live. After enjoying being at St. Peter Live, eating and having a few drinks on the ride home Justice ask Shelia can they do this again, Shelia with yes. Shelia going on to say she sincerely had fun and had never felt this good in a long time with all the troubles that had transpired in her life.

After that date Justice and Shelia were together all the time, Justice getting to know Zoie. This one-day Justice, Hakeem, and Marcus were hanging, and Justice had this glow, this joy, this satisfaction on his face, Hakeem express to Justice, Shelia got that glow on his face, and Marcus with a little laughter looking at Hakeem saying Laken has the same glow on his face.

Justice saying he cannot imagine not having Shelia and Zoie in his life. Hakeem looking at Justice and saying thanks, Justice ask thanks for what, and Hakeem explaining for being good to his daughter. Justice giving Hakeem a handshake saying no problem, no problem at all.

Marcus giving Justice and Hakeem handshakes expressing they are some lucky fellows because Stacy, Shelia, and Laken are some special ladies to be around, they are real, their conversation is real to hear.

Chapter Fourteen

To Know

Frank sitting in his office coughing when Kelly walks in, Kelly asking Frank is he okay. Frank conveying, he is feeling kind of ill. Kelly pleading to Frank she knows how he do not like going to the doctor, but she is going to take him to the doctor, no questions asked.

Kelly surprise with Frank response of okay. Kelly looking in the yellow pages finding a doctor a city blocks down the street from the warehouse, so Kelly takes Frank to doctor. Once in the office the receptionist gives Frank some paperwork to fill out. Frank going sitting down beside Kelly filling out the paper, then taking the paperwork back to the receptionist. The receptionist saying the doctor will be with him shortly. Frank coughing the more going sitting beside Kelly.

The nurse comes get Frank taking him to a room, checking his blood pressure, than the nurse saying the doctor will be right in. Soon after the Doctor comes into the room, she ask Frank what's the problem, Frank explaining he got this cough he can't get rid of, and it getting worse.

The doctor pulls out a small light out of her jacket asking Frank to open his mouth, shining the light down his throat, then saying he can close his mouth. After checking his throat, the doctor explaining to Frank she is going to have some test ran. The doctor writes a prescription for Frank, then the doctor leaves the room, as the nurse comes into the room taking Frank to have some tests ran.

After the tests were ran the nurse explaining as soon as the results comes back they will get in touch with him. Frank and Kelly leaves the doctor's office going and having his prescription filled. Afterward Frank with this depressing filling ask Kelly to take him home.

The Tests Results

A week later the tests results came back, and the receptionist calls Frank asking him if he can come to the office as soon as he can. Frank did not like the sound of that, but saying to the receptionist okay, he is on his way. Once he made it to the doctor's office, the doctor comes out front, and when the doctor sees Frank, she ask him to come into her office.

Frank looking at the doctor with this serious look on his face saying, lay it on him doc, as Frank coughing harder. The doctor communicate she is sorry to tell him this, but he has stage four lung cancer, and there is nothing that can be done, but to keep him on the medicine that she has prescribed, for the next few months.

Frank asking the doctor what she is telling him is he only have a few months to live. The doctor expressing, yes, she wish he had come to her a lot earlier, and they could have done something about this. Frank teary eyes replies, he wishes he had come too. Frank going on to say he did not like going to the doctor, nor has ever thought of getting a checkup.

After leaving the doctor's office, Frank goes to David's office, and David's secretary not knowing him asks, may she help him. Frank asking, he needs to see David. She asks do he have an appointment, Frank saying no, he do not have an appointment. Frank expressing David is his brother, the secretary saying all right, calling David saying his brother is here to see him. David replying okay, send him into his office. Once Frank comes into David office, for the first time looking around saying this is nice.

Frank explaining the reason for the visit he wants him to know before the rest of the family, and he going to get right to the point. David, with this concern, look asking Frank what's going on. Frank teary eyes utter he got stage four lung cancer, and he do not have much time longer to live. David concern look turn to sadness saying no, no this cannot be true. Frank expressing, yes it is true and he does not have long to live.

David gets up from his desk with tears, going around to Frank giving him a hug saying he is so sorry. David and Frank get on their knees, Frank praying, please forgive him Heavenly Father, for his selfishness, his way of thinking, his way of living wanting everything fast, knowing everything too fast want last, yet still wanting everything fast.

Frank goes home and lay down on the couch falling asleep dreaming of his death. Frank's spirit in waiting looking into the abyss, seeing a bottomless pit, and when an angel comes to his spirit asking why should his soul have the privilege to even get to the gates of Heaven to plead his case to rest his soul in Heaven.

The angel goes on to say to Frank's spirit, let them look over the life given to him with free will, and see the choices made. Frank awaken in a sweat getting off the couch, getting on his knees praying, asking forgiveness of his sins, his way of thinking life should be, to know what was right, but still doing what was wrong.

Frank gets off his knees teary eyes shouting who wants to go knowing the time has come to leave, only now having repentance, only now, only now while on death's bed.

Plans for the Funeral

Charle, Sarah, and Kelley they got with the pastor of the family church, plus made plans with the funeral director. The funeral a week from now, on a Saturday. After they left the church, Charle ask Sarah and Kelly are they hungry. Sarah express yes, Charle looking at Kelly saying he is going to take her to this place called The Soul Food Place, and it is one of the best soul food restaurants in the county and in the state. Kelly smiling saying okay let go eat.

Once in the restaurant, the first thing Ms. Powell saying, she is sorry for their lost, then she shouts how the hell are yawl. Then she looks hard at Kelly shouts oh my! Trouble, trouble and more trouble, Ms. Powell starts laughing, saying to Kelly she doesn't remember her, but she was her mother best friend, and she used to babysit her when she was a little girl. Ms. Powell goes on to say looking at Kelley, her heart was broken when her mother passed away, and Ms. Powell asking Kelley how is her little brother, and his name. Kelly giving Ms. Powell a hug, and saying his name is Hakeem, and he is doing well. Ms. Powell expressing that is great, and give him a hug for her.

After eating at The Soul Food Place, Kelly give Ms. Powell her number, giving her another hug, saying she will be back to visit, but if she ever needs anything call her. Kelly giving Charle and Sarah a hug, saying she was headed back to the city, to the warehouse to see what Frank had going on, so she can make sure everything is in order.

On the drive back to the city Kelly broke down remembering Frank telling her the story about when he first met her. How he was sitting in his car in front of the Bin-Over waiting for David. How when Daid made it there the both of them had gotten out of their cars. David gave him a handshake saying he was sorry knowing he was a little late. Then they walked into the Bin-Over and got a table close to the stage, and ordering some drinks when the DJ announced Chocolate Beauty was coming to the stage.

Kelly with a smile remembering she was Chocolate Beauty, how she dance, and after she had gotten off the stage, she and Frank made eye contact. How Frank paid for her to lap dances with him the rest of the night.

Kelly now back at the warehouse when she walks into Franks's office the first person she sees is Hakeen sitting in Frank's chair. She look at Hakeem asking what is he doing sitting in Frank's office and in Frank's chair. Hakeen explaining he knows the operation, and he can bring Marcus along with him, plus Justice to run the operation.

Kelley saying okay giving him a hug, saying this hug is coming from this old lady, name Ms. Powell, she was best friend with mom. Hakeem saying that what is up, going to say is she for real about him running the warehouse. Kelley smiling, expressing that was the plan all along. Frank had paperwork done leaving you the warehouse. Hakeem now with a tear, expressing he is so sorry Frank was gone, and he will make him proud. Kelly with a tear saying she know he will walking out of the office.

Hakeem called Marcus saying he wants him in the game with him and Justice. Hakeem explaining Kelley has given him the operation to the warhouse. Marcus yells over the phone alright, and Hakeem saying word up!

Marcus getting off the phone when Stacy ask him do he want to ride with her and Shelia to pick up Justic from the detention center. Marcus is so happy knowing he is back in the game, saying yes, that will great. Marcus, Stacy, and Shelia all were waiting at the gate of detention center to pick up Justice. Justice walking out, and Shelia jumps out of the car and ran up to Justice, hugging and kissing him.

Stacy and Marcus got out of the car. Stacy gave Justice a hug and Marcus gave Justice a handshake. Marcus asks Justice what do he wants to do, and Justice saying, eat, drink, and be merry.

As they are driving off Hakeem calls Marcus asking have he pick up Justice yet. Marcus saying yes, he is in the car with him now. Hakeem ask to put Justice on the phone, Marcus giving Justice his phone, and Hakeem saying what's up cuzs going on to say a free man, asking is he ready to collaborate with him a Marcus running the warehouse. Justice hollering for real, Hakeem saying for real. Justice shouts yes after getting off the phone, giving Marcus his phone back. Marcus pulls over the car goes to the trunk and gets a bottle of Cognac XO he had bought for Justice, asking everyone to get out of the car and drink a shot for Frank.

Everyone got out of the car drinking a shot for Frank, and after the shot. Marcus pours the rest of the bottle on the ground saying rest in peace Frank.

The Funeral

Sallie, Alvin, Shirley, Lewis, Sarah, Charles, David, Grace, Kelley,' Jesse, Mellody, Barbara, Jim, Tina, Larry, Hakeem, Laken, Justice, Sheila, Marcus, and Stacy. Were all at the funeral.

They all gathered in the church as the preacher walk to the pulpit saying let not your heart be trouble, Jesus have prepared a place for us. The pastor looking at the congregation, saying let not be the only reason to meet in church with tears of sadness, lets meet in church for tears of joy.

The pastors asking for amen, the congregation saying amen. The pastor pause wiping his forehead with his handkerchief. Then the pastor saying he know Frank lived a fast life, but in the end he call him asking him for his forgiveness, and the pastor saying he is not the one to be asking for forgiveness. The pastor shouted it is God's forgiveness he should be asking for. The pastor shouted the more how he and Frank prayed, and prayed, and how Frank repented for his sins, now asking the congregation can he get an amen. Charles and Sarah shouted the loudest amen.

Chapter Fifteen

Years After College

Laken graduating in the arts, she went to law school then graduating from law school in flying colors. She is now a certified lawyer and hoping to achieve every one of her dreams and what her heart desires with the choice of this profession.

After Laken graduating from law school Barbara and Tina wanted her to come and work at the firm, but Laken had other plans. She decided and got a job as a public defender, plus working with the inter-city youths she felt this would be an avenue to touch lives of the black youth.

Laken was up against the lifestyle, of some of the youth, the trade of hard drugs, and the indulgence in criminal activities for means of survival. Other youth live a life of poverty, yet to live with the love of the mother, but the negligence of the father. The fatherless child, a child with a life of pain, frustration, and abandonment only to know welfare was a monthly way to live.

To live a scared life of the blue, the mistreatment of some of the blue thinking all young Black men were the same. How they treated young Black men as though they had no place to live on this earth, and if they did it was in jail on trump up charges putting young black men into the system.

Laken all she wanted was to make the lives of the youth from the inner-city better by defending them, plus putting in the minds of others, other with power, others who could make a different, that the youth of the inter-city were not looking for a handout, but a chance. A chance as anyone who dreams to live a good life, not a life that could be a life of a nightmare.

Laken knew it was an uphill battle for the inter-city youths from the Windy City to Hotlanta, the wars in the neighborhood, the dealing with the sound of gun shots everywhere, stealing, killing, and people dying because of being involve directly or indirectly.

Laken realized there were no jobs on any corner for the unemployed inter-city youths, yet liquor stores on every corner. With this in mind, Laken decided to run for city council hoping she could get the votes that would be needed so she could help end these wars in these neighborhoods.

Laken campaigned thoroughly, with Paige, Stacy, Shelia, and the rest of the family helping her. They created an awareness with the tag "Rehabilitation." She wanted people in the community to know the next council person elected would solely focus on the people's general interest and not that of personal interest or selfishness.

Laken she won, she became city councilwoman for the district of the community. She became the voice of the people, the people with the invisible voices which screamed for help yet were purposefully ignored. Her voice became that of wounded hearts and souls, she became the opening for the changes that were about to take place soon.

Laken voice was to bring jobs to the community, no more destruction of lives in the community, no more drugs in the community, no more chaos and problems as usual, as she was about the opportunity to be heard, as her voice was for the mayor of the city to hear, not just part of the city, but the whole city.

Laken had a real passion for the job she was doing in the city, but she knew something was missing, and she could not figure it out until that morning, when she laid her eyes on Hakeem. She realized how deeply she felt for him, but she is knew his lifestyle was not the lifestyle for her, nor her purpose.

They got to talking catching up on many things that had gone on in their lives since the last time they saw one another. Hakeem telling Laken he is legit, he is out of the game, he sold Frank's Warehouse to Marcus, and he bought the Bin-Over from Kelly, this put a good feeling on Laken's heart.

Hakeem explain this to Laken, he knew the only way he could have her in his life was to become legit, and since she has been in college, to now a city councilwoman that all he has been doing is working on becoming legit. Hakeem goes on to say looking at Laken with hope on his face, he always knew he wanted her in his life.

Laken ask can they talk later, asking Hakeem for his phone. Hakeem reaching in his pocket getting his phone giving it to Laken, and Laken programming her number in, asking Hakeem to call her sometime, Hakeem taking his phone saying he surely will.

Laken was on her way to look at this building which could be of good use for the inter-city youth. The building was an old recreational building with a cafeteria but needed a lot of work. She had talked with some of the parents to volunteer working in the cafeteria to help prepare meals for the youth who had nothing to eat before and after school hours.

Hakeem was headed to this shopping center to look for new furniture for his office in the Bin-Over. Hakeem riding feeling good about the conversation he just had with Laken thinking to himself he can't wait to give her a call, he can't wait the start of something new, the game was over, and he was legit. Hakeem pulls in the shopping center parking lot sitting there for a minute reminiscing, and then he left thinking he can wait.

The Take Over

Paige had graduated with honors in criminal justice, she finally had an idea of the law and how to respond to and defend cases, she became Assistance DA, and later the DA Paige and reunite with Kim when she starts working with the DA office on narcotics cases.

Kim was investigating Marcus, not letting Paige know anything knowing Paige might mentioned something to Marcus about Kim investigating this big-time drug dealer. Paige notices how Kim acted differently with her when it came to talking about Marcus and she was wondering what did Marcus do. Marcus helps in the inner city with elderly people needing grocery, plus once a year giving out computer to some inter-city kids.

Paige refused to think Marcus was a drug dealer. He is in charge of the warehouse that Frank left for Hakeem. Paige thinking he was making the money he was making because he and Hakeem are the best of friends. Still the change in Kim about Marcus, Paige started thinking, it was Hakeem. Hakeem was the drug dealer and Kim knew Marcus and Hakeem were close.

Paige call Marcus asking was he busy, and Marcus saying he can be available for her. Paige saying she going get straight to the point is Hakeem selling drugs out of the warehouse.

Marcus laugh asking why would she ask that. Paige explain to Marcus Kim think he is selling drugs out of the warehouse. Marcus expresses that she can keep thinking that because all he is doing is making a living.

Marcus thoughts were what if Kim was on to him. Marcus called Valarie who he had retain, Valarie was recommend to him from her brother Justice. Valarie answered Marcus call, and Marcus asks Valarie can they meet somewhere.

Valarie express lunch time at the Rooftop restaurant, Marcus with okay. Lunch time Marcus pulls up to the restaurant giving the valet the keys to his new Mercedes-Benz G 63AMG, and about a few minutes later Kim pulls up giving the valet her keys to her Mercedes-Benz S 580.

Valarie and Marcus take the elevator to the rooftop to the restaurant sitting at the bar. Marcus ordering two double shots of Cognac XO. Then both ordering stakes Valarie well done and Marcus medium well. While sipping on their drinks Marcus explains he thinks he is being investigated. Valarie asks why do he think that. Marcus expressing, he heard something from someone that this detective Kim is investigating a big-time- drug dealer in the city.

Valarie laughs asking Marcus how many big-time-drug dealers he think is in the city. Marcus smile saying this detective Kim went to high school with him and she had always suspected him of selling weed, even though he did not. Valarie said okay she will have her investigator to find out what is going on with this Kim.

Even though Marcus was understanding what Valarie had told him, he was scared, he felt Kim knew too much about him. When Marcus left the restaurant he goes to a locker at the airport, leaving an envelope with cash in it, a note with Kim's name and information, with the word half, meaning the other half after the job was done.

Marcus learning this level of the game from Hakeem who told him the standard for a hitman. There was no need for contact the hitman, the hitman knew what to do once he check the locker. The hitman knew to check the locker once a month, knowing that only a few had a key to the locker.

A month later, Marcus was watching something on television, and Breaking News come across the T.V. screen saying Officer Kim stabbed to death in the line of duty for a robbery gone wrong, suspect apprehended. Marcus knew this was an excellent job because they had a suspect, knowing it was not the hitman. Marcus then goes to the locker and leaves the other half of the money in the locker.

Marcus back at home watching the news seeing Paige, stun trying to hold her emotion, and telling news reporters that they will go for the maxes on this killer. The news reporters asking all sorts of questions about the person in custody. Paige saying Hakeem is the suspect, Paige then leaves the reporters getting with the detective over the case asking her to get all the evidence she can come up with.

Marcus hearing Hakeem name thinking to himself how can this be, so he goes to Laken given her a lot of cash to represent Hakeem letting her know there is no way Hakeem could have done this. This makes Laken feel the more better hearing Marcus telling her Hakeem could not have done this.

Laken goes to the jail telling the officers she needs to see her client, the man accused of killing a fellow officer. She was escorted to a holding room, and waiting for them to bring out Hakeem.

Once Hakeem with a black eyes, puff lips was brought to the holding room, Laken looking at Hakeem with sorrow on her face expressing she know he didn't do this because of the conversation they had. Laken then expressed that she needs to get some information, and Hakeem with sadness in his voice saying whatever information he can provide he will.

Laken asking Hakeem where was he at the time of the stabbing. Hakeen explains he had gotten out of his car, and this man bump into him. Laken ask Hakeem did he notice how the man look, Hakeen saying no because about that time people were running everywhere, and he did not know what was going, so he started running too. Then a police officer tackle him finding a knife in his suit jacket.

Laken explains she is going to get his preliminary hearing as soon as possible. As the guard took Hakeem back to his cell, Laken leaving going back to her office not knowing what to think. Later that day, Paige calls Laken, saying, she know she care for Hakeem, but a police killer. Laken lack of words, but Paige going on to say she can't believe her she thought she was better than this hanging up the phone.

Six Months Later

The preliminary hearing Laken give the judge a motion to grant her client bail, and Paige counters the motion that the suspect is a flight risk. The judge looks at Laken saying bail denied, reason as the prosecutor said, plus it would not be safe out there for an accused police killer. The judge looks at her calendar, saying a trial date will be set for six months from this day at nine am. Courts adjourn.

Once Paige gets back to her office, she calls up the detectives on the case, asking her to get more evidence to find out if any witnesses saw anything that they are missing. In the meantime, Laken thinking she needs to find if anyone saw Hakeem getting out of his car about the time of the murder because this is the only way she can prove his innocence.

Laken calls Valarie asking her do she know any good investigator, Valarie express yes, she knows this great investigator who knows the streets. Valarie saying she will have him to call her, and it on her, no charge because she believes Hakeem is innocent. Valarie goes on to say no family of her would do such a thing, Laken express yes, but she did not know Hakeem was related to her. Valarie saying he is her first cousin.

This made Laken feel the better getting off the phone with Valarie, and ten minutes later Laken getting a call from Cooper saying Valarie wanted him to call her. Cooper expressing, he knows the case and he is on it, getting off the phone. Cooper on the job digging for more information finding out from a source deep with news from the underworld what goes on, on the streets of the city. The news Cooper got was there was a hit on Kim.

This person Cooper knew from the underworld telling him Kim had gotten too close to someone that she could expose. Cooper calls Laken back saying he will be at her office in an hour to give her some details he knows.

The detectives working on the case for the DA comes back to Paige with information that it was a hit on Kim. The detectives explains that there is knowledge of a witness, and the detective looks at Paige hard saying Jesse her father was the witness seeing Hakeem getting out of his car at the time of the murder.

The detective she goes on to say Jesse saw this man bumping into Hakeem putting something in his pocket. Jesse thinking it was a transaction between Hakeem and that person.

Paige order DNA and fingerprints on the knife, when the result came back, none of Hakeem DNA, nor fingerprints were on the knife. Paige understood how the city's underworld worked, and the information from the underworld could be the best information to solve crime in the city.

Paige knew with no DNA, no fingerprints, plus learning there was a hit on Kim. Paige drops the charge of murder on Hakeem, and telling the reporter there is no DNA or fingerprints, plus a credible witness saw Hakeem at the time of the murder her father, Jesse.

Marcus phone buzz Breaking News, the charges of murder have been drop on Hakeem, at the same time Laken getting the news while Cooper is in her office giving her the details of the information he had gotten.

Laken rush to the jailhouse to be there when Hakeem got release, to answer all the questions the reporters were going to ask. Once Laken made it to the jailhouse and Hakeem was released, and after Laken answering all the questions the reporters ask Hakeem. She hugs him asking do he want to go home.

Chapter Sixteen

The Decision of Love

Jill the detective taking Kim place getting Kim's information on Marcus, she goes to Paige. Paige with this heavy heart, the loss of Kim, and now she has to go to the grand jury to get a formal accusation on Marcus for being over the drug game. A week later the grand jury indicted Marcus.

Paige heavy hearted calls Marcus late in the day while he, Stacy, Shelia, and Justice are together at this nice restaurant celebrating Justice asking Shelia to marry him. Paige telling Marcus he has been indicted on drug charges, Marcus getting off the phone with this look of concernment. Stacy seeing this look asking him why the concern look, and who was that on the phone.

Marcus smile saying it is nothing, and it was Paige calling him to tell Justice and Shelia congratulation. Marcus telling Justice and Shelia, Paige said congratulation, and after Marcus not wanting to be a distraction he order a bottle of the best champagne.

After they had celebrated Marcus ask Justice and Shelia can they give Stacy a ride home. Stacy looking at Marcus knowing it was much more to that call from Paige, thinking of that concern look that was on Marcus's face. Justice saying okay, Stacy express she will see him when he gets home.

Marcus getting into his car, he calls Valarie, and Valarie express she heard, plus she is on the case. After Marcus getting off the phone with Valarie, he starts shouting saying take it, take it all, he do not want it anymore, he do not want the greed of money, the lust of power, the guilt of Kim's death he carry. Marcus hitting the steering wheel shouting the more, saying take it, and whatever price he have to pay he will pay.

During this time Alfonso transferring from Atlanta jail to prison, and as soon as get got to prison these guys are trying to jump on him, but Rosco seeing what was happening. Rosco had the respected of the prison yard, plus the guards, so Rosco and his crew saying no, not today, nor any other day.

Alfonso is like thanks, Rosco asking Alfonso what part of Georgia he is from, Alfonso saying Atlanta, Rosco laughs saying where. Alfonso saying okay he is from Dawton Georgia. This open Rosco eye the wider asking who is his peoples. Alfonso said his Father was Frank, and before Alfonso can say anything else, Rosco asking Alfonso, Frank was his father.

Alfonso saying yes, Rosco with a big smile saying they are family, and he was like an uncle to Frank, how they use to go pick up moonshine for Old man Perkins. Wow! Alfonso shouted then asking was he the one who took the rap for his father. Rosco saying yes, at that time Frank was old enough to go to prison, but still too young.

This got Alfonso to thinking how he heard Marcus is being indicted, so he gets in touch with Valarie to come visit him. Valarie making the drive to Macon Georgia, once Valarie was process in, Alfonso lets Valarie know he wants to make a deal with Paige about Marcus not knowing anything about the disturbing of drugs out of the warehouse. Valarie is surprised, but she asks Alfonso what deal he wants from Paige. Alfonso asking to get his time reduce for the years he had done in jail, plus the information he will tell her about the distribution of drugs from the warehouse cannot be used against him, and he wants this in writing.

Valarie leaves the prison, and she goes to Paige's office, Paige sitting behind her desk when Valarie walks in, Valarie ask can she have a seat. Paige is like sure, Valarie sitting down, Paige asks Valarie what can she help her with, Paige with this look of disarray on her face asking do her cousin wants to make a plea deal. Valarie with a smile saying no, but she knows someone who do.

Paige is like who!!! Who wants to make a plea deal on this case for Marcus, no, she is not going to let anyone take the fall for Marcus as much as she loves him. Valarie smile became the more bigger saying she just left visiting Alfonso, and he said if he can get a plea for time served, and no more time for the information he wants to give, put it in writing and he will give all the information she needs on how the warehouse ran.

Paige is like why would she make a deal with Alfonso, Valarie stops smiling expressing because Alfonso said Marcus knows nothing about the distribution of drugs out of the warehouse. Valarie looks at Paige with this serious look asking her do she wants to put her family in prison. Paige now teary eyes saying no.

Paige express to Valarie she will have some papers written up for Alfonso for time served, and no more time if he can give her the information needed about the warehouse. Paige then goes on to say if Alfonso don't give her the information she needs, not only will she put Marcus under the jail, but Alfonso will never see the light of day.

The next day Paige had the paperwork written up asking Valarie to get the paperwork, once in Paige's office Paige gives Valarie the paperwork looking at her saying if she do not get everything she needs to know on paper, and recorded from Alfonso all this paperwork is nothing but trash. Valarie taking the paperwork saying okay, she is on her way to Macon to see Alfonso, and she will have everything she need back to her tomorrow.

Valarie leaves the office going to Macon, and once there processing into the prison. Valarie with the paperwork for Alfonso to read and sign, plus a recorder, and paper for Alfonso to write, and record how the drug game work from the warehouse. Alfonso reading the paperwork then asking Valarie for a pin, Valarie giving him a pin, he signs the paperwork.

After Alfonso signs the paperwork he started writing and talking while Valarie is recording him. Alfonso writing, talking with before Marcus came to work at the warehouse his father Frank was over the drug game, and he learn him everything, but because he stayed into much trouble, so when his father died, giving Hakeem paperwork to run the warehouse, and Hakeem hired Marcus to be a manager. Alfonso goes on to say Hakeem nor Marcus did not know what was going on in the warehouse because he ran it from his jail cell.

As Alfonso is talking, writing saying Marcus had no clue what he was getting into, how the goods coming through the warehouse seem to be legit, but nothing was legit, even the invoices were not legit, and the only way Marcus could know is to have come to the warehouse floor and check the product, and he never did, only managing from the office.

Alfonso stops writing and starts laughing still being recorded saying Marcus was not, nor is smart enough to run drugs that were coming out of the warehouse, it take someone with heart, the love of the game of selling drugs, the love of money. Alfonso talking the more and laughing the harder, saying Marcus never had the love of selling drugs, nor the love of making money.

Alfonso said that is all he got, and Valarie she stops recording, Valarie asking Alfonso to sign the paperwork he has written, and she will get back with him, after she find out what's Paige decision is. Alfonso said no problem he is not going anywhere.

Valarie leaving the prison and on her ride home from Macon to Atlanta, she knew half of what Alfonso was saying can't be true because Marcus retain her, for a reason. Then Valarie smiles thinking the price of being a defense lawyer

The next day Valarie goes to Paige's office, Paige sitting on the couch in her office reading something when Valarie comes in her office giving Paige all the paperwork, plus the recording. After Paige takes the paperwork, looking at Valarie with this look of hopelessness, Paige asking Valarie is it even worth reading, or listening to the recording.

Valarie shaking her head saying it's worth both, but to listen to Alfonso talk he got to be telling the truth because he puts the on himself, and his father, Frank, who ran the drug game out of the warehouse. Paige with her eyes wide open asking Valarie Frank was Alfonso's Farther. Valarie shaking her head as to say yes, then Paige starts playing the recording, as she is reading what Alfonso had written, and afterward all she could do was to believe everything Alfonso was saying.

Negro Love

Paige telling Valarie she will drop all charges against Marcus, and Alfonso is a free man. Valarie and Paige shake hands, Valarie leaves the office, while Paige with tears of joy, glad she does not have to go through with prosecuting Marcus. Valarie get to her car, and she calls Marcus saying Paige is dropping the charges, and he have Alfonso to thanks this for.

Marcus is at awe, asking what does Alfonso have to do with this, Valarie with excitement saying Alfonso gave up the operation, saying it was his father only knowing. Marcus is excited saying he cannot believe Alfonso would do something like that, Valarie said well he did.

Valarie driving to Macon with the paperwork to have Alfonso release, and once she was at the prison to have Alfonso process out, Alfonso so happy saying before he leaves he need to see Rosco. The guard taking Alfonso to sees Rosco on the yard, he give him a big hug saying thanks for everything, and all Rosco express, was Negro Love.

Bobby Shaw

Thank you for reading Negro Love, I truly hope you like it, and if you did can you do me a favor tell someone about Negro Love, and can you go to the bookstore on Amazon, and give me a review, also My next two Books will be out soon, Why Me, and Yesteryear till Tomorrow. God bless you all!!!

Made in the USA
Columbia, SC
26 July 2024